MW01058312

"The 'need' to be th[in] girls, and Laura L. Sm[ith] debut teen novel with [...] going to relate to Melissa and her struggle to 'look good'"
—MELODY CARLSON, best-selling Christian author

"Melissa is a vibrant teen who teaches readers signs of an eating disorder and the value of spirituality in working through the treatment. *Skinny* is powerful because it heightens the awareness of eating disorders—the key to early diagnosis and treatment, which translates to improved adolescent wellness. Thank you, Laura Smith, for empowering young women!"
—DR. MICHELLE NAEGELE, former chief of staff, McCullough Hyde Memorial Hospital

"Adolescent readers will appreciate this true-to-life account of the ambivalence, pain, and emotional struggle of living with an eating disorder. The seemingly 'normal' drive to achieve, win the favor of a young man, and please one's parents is captured in a readable text that does not underplay the real consequences and health risks that accompany eating disorders. The importance of spiritual connection, not always portrayed in similar stories, is an added bonus."

—JULIE CAMPBELL-RUGGAARD, PhD, LPCC, RN

"A real story for real girls. If you've ever felt over-whelmed by schoolwork, relationships, your friends, or activities, you need to read this book."

—HEATHER GEMMEN WILSON, best-selling author

Skinny

She was starving to fit in...

Status Updates
Originally published by NavPress, 2008

Cover design by: Angela-Designs.com
Cover photography by: Kelci Alane Photography

This novel is a work of fiction. Names, characters, places, and incidents are either the product of the author's imagination or are used fictitiously. Any resemblance to actual events, locales, organizations, or persons, living or dead, is entirely coincidental and beyond the intent of either the author or publisher.

Unless otherwise identified, all Scripture quotations in this publication are taken from the Holy Bible: New International Version (NIV). Copyright c 1973, 1978, 1984, by International Bible Society. Used by permission of Zondervan Publishing House. All rights reserved.

Summary: When the pressures of having good grades, friends, a position on the dance team, and a boyfriend become too much for Melissa, she turns to disordered eating to attempt to regain control.

ISBN-10: 0-991152581
ISBN-13: 978-0-9911525-8-2

[Anorexia nervosa—Fiction, Eating Disorder—Fiction, Self image—Fiction, Dance—Fiction, High school—Fiction, Dating—Fiction. Christian life—Fiction, Romance—Fiction.]

This book is for Tina, Kristen, Carrie, and anyone struggling with an eating disorder. I carry your stories around in my heart. Remember that God made you in His image, and therefore, you are beautiful.

Acknowledgments

Thank You to God for making the words flow from my fingertips. Thank You for the characters, the stories, the ideas You pop into my head and for the gift of writing. I pray both my writing and my life serve You.

To my husband, Brett: Without you I would have never taken fingers to keys. Thank you for believing in me. Thank you for encouraging me. Thank you for being my cheerleader. But thank you mostly for loving me. This writer's endless supply of words is not enough to thank you for being my partner in life or to express the expanse of my love for you.

To my M&Ms, Maddie, Max, Mallory, and Maguire: You fill my days with inspiration, giggles, snuggles, and a constant reminder of God's love. I love you as big as the ocean!

To everyone at NavPress, especially Rebekah Guzman: Thank you for believing in the importance of Melissa's story and for believing in me.

To my editors, Amy Parker and Kathy Mosier: Thank you for enhancing, strengthening, and finessing my writing. You make it better than I ever could. Without you, *Skinny* would be scrawny.

To my mom, Becca, and Bethany: Thank you for reading various parts of this manuscript in its working stages. Your comments helped guide Melissa where she needed to go.

Chapter One

Melissa posed as perfectly as a marble statue. Her head bent at a forty-five degree angle, her fingers spread equidistantly, rigid, and exactly in line with her thighs. The music pulsed in her veins. She inhaled and silently counted along with Todd.

"Five, six, seven, eight."

Even though he was only five foot five, Todd had a booming voice that commanded the attention of every girl in the room. The rhythm of the music vibrated from the speakers on the church's glossy gymnasium floor.

Like a marionette brought to life by invisible strings, Melissa jerked her hands up, forming a V with her arms, snapped her head upright, and flashed a radiant smile.

"And turn, six, seven, eight. Lift and lift and slide and slide," Todd continued like a metronome. The pulsating beat pulled Melissa's body back and forth.

Abruptly, Todd's solid muscular body relaxed. The coach turned his back to the group of girls and padded across the wooden floor to turn off the music. Since dance team was somewhere low on the priority list of varsity sports at Spring Hill High, they were allotted zero gymnasium time for practices. The school's gym was designated for the football players, the basketball players, the track team, and the softball team, but not the dance team. Luckily, the church Melissa's family attended allowed the girls to practice in their gym.

"Okay, any questions? No? Good. Then let's continue." Todd's dark skin shone with perspiration as he flawlessly demonstrated the next sequence. Tiny yellow beads woven into the ends of his cornrows bounced lightly against his strong shoulders, bulging from his gray tank top. His compact body moved effortlessly across the floor while his chocolate eyes kept constant contact with the team.

Melissa replayed his every move in her head, trying to make his motions and words translate into her body's executing the dance correctly.

Feet pounded the floor. Arms stretched to the ceiling. Hips swayed.

Melissa turned to the left.

Everyone else turned to the right.

Melissa missed bumping into Jill by a fraction of an inch. Jill was a junior who could kick higher than the rest of the team and had an attitude to match. Jill's flawless pale skin and sleek black hair were reminiscent of Snow White, but Jill certainly didn't act like a fairy-tale princess. Jill shot Melissa a glare from her bright green eyes that could have come from an evil stepmother.

Flames of shame pinched Melissa's nose and ears. She caught her breath and stumbled to get back in step. How many of the others had seen her screw up? The other girls looked so pretty, so thin, so together. Melissa felt bulky and conspicuous, like an elephant stomping across the gym. *Feel the music*, she told herself.

"Okay. That's all for today," Todd said between gulps of bottled water. "Not bad, but we have a lot to learn, ladies. We perform in two days." Todd wiped drops of water from his manicured mustache.

"Oh, and, girls, no cake between now and Friday. You want to look spectacular in your uniforms." He winked.

Sweat slid down Melissa's forehead and stung her eyes. She tried to shrink inside her T-shirt. She darted for her dance bag, grabbed it, and walked as fast as she could until she was safe behind the girls' room door. Protected by the wooden barrier, she pulled on her sweatshirt and yoga pants and exhaled.

Finally her cumbersome body, the one that had turned the wrong way, the one Todd was clearly making the cake comment about, was covered. Tears threatened to escape from her eyes. Melissa waved her hand in front of her face in an attempt to fan her embarrassment and anger away. She peered into the full-length mirror and groaned at her reflection.

Melissa slid into a stall and shut the door. She'd read about girls who threw up to lose weight. Melissa had thought about doing it before but never had the guts. How exactly should she do it? How would she position her body?

Melissa knelt in front of the white toilet. Thankfully, her yoga pants provided a thin barrier between her knees and the germs and sludge on the once-white tiled floor. The stench of urine almost made her gag. She wouldn't need to do much. Looking down at her hand, Melissa stuck out her index and middle fingers, ready to plunge them down her throat. Those two fingers could empty her of this feeling.

Squeak! The bathroom door swung open.

"Mel, is that you?" Lindsey asked.

"Uh-huh." Melissa felt her face burn with shame. She tried to stand and turn as silently as possible, then swung open the door.

"Do you think there's any way I'll get this routine down by Friday night?" Lindsey rolled her eyes and smiled. The girls had met only about three months ago when they both made the Spring Hill High dance team. They had gone to different grade schools but had bonded immediately. They were inseparable at practice.

Lindsey was Melissa's physical opposite: five one and so tiny she could still buy her clothes from the kids' department. Her blonde curls framed her pretty face and her pale blue eyes, which sparkled when she spoke. She looked like one of Melissa's dolls she had dressed and fed when she was younger.

Melissa was five nine. She usually wore her straight dark brown hair pulled back into a ponytail revealing her round face, forest green eyes, and the freckles that spotted her nose. Friends told her she was slender, but she described herself as "medium-sized."

"You'll get it, Linds. You're basically awesome."

"Hardly. I'm lucky to have even made this team." Lindsey pushed open the restroom door with her back.

"Right," Melissa began. "I was the one who almost fell flat on my face. Todd moves so fast."

Just then, Jill sauntered through the door as if Lindsey were opening it for her.

"Nice turns." She nodded toward Melissa.

"Nice makeup," Lindsey whispered when they were out of earshot in the hallway, commenting on Jill's overdone face. Lindsey looked around to make sure no one was listening, then gave Melissa a silent high five and whispered, "I don't care what Jill thinks. We rock."

Melissa tried to imitate Lindsey's confidence, but she was still humiliated by her misstep, and her hands shook from almost being caught in the bathroom. *Rock* was not a word to describe her, unless, of course, it was the round, heavy kind.

Chapter Two

Melissa shuffled into French class the next morning as the bell vibrated in her ears. There were no assigned seats in Monsieur Renauld's class, but everyone sat in the same seats every day anyway. Melissa always sat in the second row all the way to the right. She could reach out and touch the whiteboard Monsieur Renauld used to post special notices. But today someone was sitting in her seat.

A boy she didn't recognize sat in her regular chair that was next to her best friend since second grade, Gracie. The stranger had square shoulders that looked like the bottom side of a triangle and dark, shiny hair that curled around his ears and the back of his neck. The seat immediately behind him was vacant because Jamal was absent today. Melissa slid into Jamal's empty wooden seat and caught her breath.

The new kid smelled nice, like . . . soap. That was it. Soap. Not the fruity, florally, jellybean-colored soaps that Melissa and her friends bought at the Bubble Bath Boutique but good, old-fashioned, clean-smelling soap.

The boy turned and looked at her with round,

coffee-colored eyes framed by thick, dark lashes Melissa would kill for. It was as if he had sensed her smelling him.

Melissa leaned back and smiled.

He smiled back, then turned to face the front as Monsieur Renauld said, *"Bonjour, mes amis."*

"Bonjour, Monsieur Renauld," the class chanted in unison.

Melissa stole a glance at Gracie. She and Gracie knew each other better than anyone else in the world, even their parents. She knew Gracie would be thinking the same thing she was. Gracie winked a narrow, dark eye at Melissa, then flipped her head, her sleek, black bob swinging onto her shoulders.

Melissa's silver charm bracelet jingled as she inadvertently raised her left hand to her mouth and nibbled her nails.

"Class, I would like to introduce you to our new student," Monsieur Renauld's nasally voice droned. The teacher nodded toward the new boy.

Melissa pulled her hand from her mouth, disgusted at her icky habit. She didn't mean to bite her fingernails. She just did. Whenever she was bored in class, talking on the phone, or flipping through a magazine, those nubby nails seemed to end up between her teeth.

I will quit chewing my nails this instant so this cute boy won't see my stubby fingernails, she silently vowed.

"This is Beau Pointreaux. He comes to us from New Orleans."

Beau gave a weak smile and quickly sank back into his chair.

"Maintenant, nous sommes commençons avec les mots de Halloween."

Melissa's mouth formed the correct pronunciation of the French words for *ghost* and *pumpkin*. She loved French class, partly because she was good at it. The rolling syllables felt natural to her tongue, not stilted as they were for most of her classmates. She also loved the idea of France: the scenes of beautiful people impeccably dressed, strolling down charming streets, and sipping foam-capped coffees at crowded cafés. Actually, she loved all of her classes, except Chemistry. What did atoms have to do with the rest of her life anyway?

The scent of soap wafted her way again.

He is so cute! Beau Pointreaux, Beau Pointreaux, she repeated to herself.

After class Gracie grabbed Melissa's elbow with her dainty hand. "Don't let Drew hear me say it, but he is, like, so cute!" she whisper-screamed in Melissa's ear.

"I'd say *perfect*!" Melissa emphasized. "And"—she raised her eyebrows—"he smells *mmmmmm*. But it's not fair for *you* to like him. One, you already have a boyfriend, and two, you're so skinny I could never compete!"

Beau shuffled past them. Melissa and Gracie fell silent, then erupted in uncontrollable giggles.

"It doesn't seem exactly fair that he's in French class," Gracie griped. "I mean, he's French. That would be like me taking Mandarin."

"He's not from France!" Melissa laughed. "Lots of people in New Orleans have French heritage, you know, French names."

"Oh, I know. Beau Pointreaux? Poor guy. What a name. . . ." Gracie shook her head.

"Yeah, what a name," Melissa cooed. "Anyway, I'm glad he's in our class." She tucked her hair behind her ears.

"I wonder why?" Gracie grinned.

"Maybe he can tutor me." Melissa raised her eyebrows.

"Like you need a tutor, Miss Honor Student." Gracie shook her head.

"Here's me." Melissa grinned, turning toward her Algebra room.

"See ya, Yellow," Gracie called, using Melissa's nickname that had evolved from calling her Mel, then Mellow, then Mello Yello, and finally just Yellow.

"*Au revoir,* Gray," Melissa lobbed back and darted in her classroom just as the second period bell rang.

Standing next to the scrawny Mrs. Poppendeck in the front of the classroom was Beau.

Chapter Three

"*B*eat, beat, beat, beat, beat," Todd repeated as his left foot flexed and tapped the Achilles tendon on his right foot. "And twist, two, three, four."

Melissa swiveled her hips in perfect time with the music. When she was on the dance floor, there was nothing else—no school, no parents, no one to please— just music and movement. She felt the music was part of her. Her body itched to move to the notes booming from the speakers. Her adrenaline rushed, and she felt reckless and giddy.

"Okay, everyone take five while I make an announcement," said Todd dramatically, wiping the sweat from his mustache with a towel.

Melissa walked to the back of the gym and pulled a bottled water out of her bag. She cracked the seal and gulped down a third of the bottle before she came up for air. Inhaling and exhaling deeply, she smiled at Lindsey, then walked back toward Todd.

The team of girls formed a circle around the only male among them. Sweat glistened on all of their fit bodies. Some nodded or smiled, but no one spoke.

"Soooo," Todd began, "several of you ladies have been asking about officer auditions for next year." He paused to sip his water. "Anyone interested in trying out needs to let me know by the end of November." He tapped the ball of his foot on the floor, then flipped it over so the top side of his toes slapped the hard wood.

"After that, I'm on break until after Christmas. When we come back together in January, I'll start teaching the sequence on Saturday mornings at seven o'clock."

A loud groan came from everyone.

Todd smiled slyly and shifted his large brown eyes from left to right, building anticipation in his team. "You'll have all of February to practice on your own and to make sure your bodies are in perfect shape. We'll have auditions in March, right before I head to the beach for Spring Break." Todd flipped his head back like a diva. "Oh, and auditions are open to everyone."

Melissa's heart raced inside her gray T-shirt. She was only a freshman, and her body was *not* in perfect shape, but something deep inside of her craved the slot of captain, or at least lieutenant. She had always earned solos in her ballet and jazz recitals, but this was different. The girls on this team were so talented! Plus, the older girls had more experience. As far as she knew, there had never been an underclass officer before.

There were twenty girls on the team and only two slots. Of course, not everyone would try out, and the seniors would graduate, but still! Melissa wanted it so much she could taste the metallic captain's whistle in her mouth.

"Okay, enough chitchat." Todd waited for everyone to resume their places. "And five, six, here we go." He pushed play, and the notes of the electric piano echoed through the gym.

Melissa took a deep breath and prayed a silent prayer. *Dear God, I don't know why I want this so badly, but please let me get it. I'll work so hard for it. I'll do anything,* Melissa pleaded while spotting the front wall to keep from getting dizzy.

/ / /

*M*elissa slammed her door shut, blinked her eyes, and exhaled loudly as she climbed into her mom's minivan.

"Hi," she panted, out of breath.

"Hi, sweetie. Good practice today?" asked Mom, who was, as always, tastefully dressed, in khaki pants and a lavender sweater set.

"Yeah." Melissa struggled to get settled with three large cardboard boxes around her feet and her gym bag on her lap.

Click. She fastened her seat belt.

"What are those big yellow boxes?" Mom asked, tilting her head to get a better look.

"Tootsie Pops."

"Yum. Are they all for me, or did you go ahead and buy the trick-or-treat candy this year?" Mom winked.

Melissa had gotten most of her mother's genes. They had the same pine green eyes, the same freckles, and the same thick brown hair, except Mom kept hers cut in a short, sensible style, and Melissa grew hers long enough to touch her belt.

"Very funny, Mom. We have to sell them to raise money for new uniforms." Melissa repositioned the boxes. "But you could buy all of them from me as your trick-or-treat candy."

"How much are you charging?" asked Mom.

"A quarter a sucker or five for a dollar." Melissa flashed her best salesgirl grin.

"Too expensive for me." Mom waved to Pastor Al, who was walking through the church parking lot. "But I'll tell you what. I'll buy ten for our treat jar."

"That will be two dollars, please." Melissa held out her hand.

"How about I pay you when we get home, and you can pick out which flavors to fill the jar with, okay?"

"Okay."

The hum of the heater filled the car.

"Is there something else, Mel?" Mom pulled her gaze from the road to look her daughter in the eye.

"I wish they were M&M'S."

"You wouldn't have any allowance left, and you would never fit into your uniform if they were M&M'S," Mom said with a laugh. "You would eat them all yourself."

The silence surrounded them again.

Melissa reached to turn up the volume of the Third Day song coming from the speakers.

"Is there something *else*, Mel?"

Mom always knew when something was up.

"Todd announced officer tryouts today," Melissa said, tracing the designs on the Tootsie box with her index finger.

"Oh?" Mom turned the volume back down.

Melissa knew she was supposed to say more, but she was afraid to say the words out loud.

"Yeah. They're open to everyone." Melissa looked out the window, then back at Mom. "Even underclassmen."

"Are you going to try out?"

For a second Melissa couldn't breathe. She chewed on the hangnails on either side of her right thumbnail. There it was, out in the open. Was she going to try out?

"I was thinking about it. Well, I'm sure I won't be picked, but I want to try. It sounds silly, doesn't it?"

The moment of silence that followed confirmed Melissa's fears. This was foolish. Then Mom let out a sigh and put her hand on top of Melissa's. "Melissa, if this is something you really want, then you need to go for it."

"Maybe I will." Melissa nodded, relieved. "Maybe."

At bedtime Melissa pretended her pajamas were the stark white captain's uniform. She marched around her room blowing an imaginary whistle until she laughed out loud at herself. She tumbled onto her bed and pulled out the leather-bound study Bible she read each night. She opened the vellum pages to the Ten Commandments bookmark her second-grade Sunday school teacher had given her.

She read the words of Matthew 7:7: "Seek and you will find; knock and the door will be opened to you."

Here it is in print. Lord, if I ask You to make me lieutenant or maybe even captain of the team, will You give it to me? I've never wanted anything this badly. I know it sounds selfish, but I really think I could help. Oh, by the way, could You help me sell all of my Tootsie Pops too? Back to the officer thing, I could make the underclassmen feel wanted. I could start a Bible study for the girls who were interested after practice. I could . . .

Melissa drifted to sleep.

Chapter Four

*M*elissa stared at the clock: 5:53 a.m. She turned off her alarm before it rang and reluctantly peeled off her cozy covers. Classes started at seven thirty, and if she wanted to have time to get ready, eat, and stop by her locker before school started, she had to wake up even before her parents!

She showered, pulled on her pleated uniform skirt and matching sweater, and brushed her hair into a sleek ponytail. Fridays meant football games, and the dance team had to wear their uniforms with their hair pulled back to school. She loved Fridays! Melissa felt important wearing her uniform. The entire school could see she was a good dancer, that she had made the team. Did Beau know she was on the dance team?

She bounded downstairs, planning to grab a bagel before Gracie's big brother, Tanner, showed up to take her to school. Tanner was sixteen. Ever since he got his license, he had been driving Gracie and Melissa to school. Although Melissa lived close enough to walk to school, it was more fun riding with her best friend, and it was cool showing up each day in a car.

Melissa rounded the corner to the kitchen.

"Happy birthday!" Mom and Dad grinned, still in their pajamas.

The kitchen table was piled with chocolate chip pancakes, syrup, and butter. Yellow balloons and streamers hung from the brass chandelier. Three packages wrapped in crisp white paper and tied with yellow bows sat at her place.

Melissa's whole face smiled, even her eyes.

"Yummy!"

She sat down at her place and glanced at the kitchen clock and then back at the presents.

"We know you don't have much time," said Mom. "But it wouldn't be a birthday without presents and treats. You start opening, and I'll fix your plate."

Dad took a sip of coffee and nodded. He looked like he'd been awake all of two minutes. His thinning sandy hair was tousled, and his lively green eyes hid behind his thick Clark Kent–style glasses. Melissa loved those glasses. She thought they made Dad look the part of the magazine editor he was.

Melissa tore open the small package on top—a silver pom pom charm.

"I love it!" Her eyes widened as she unhooked her bracelet to add the new charm. She extended her wrist and shook it gently so the charms tinkled.

"Glad you like it." Dad nodded.

She shoved a huge bite of fluffy pancake drenched in syrup and filled with melted bits of chocolate into her mouth.

"Mom, these are so good!"

Her other boxes held jeans, a yellow sweater, and iTunes and Amazon gift cards. No cell phone. Not that she was expecting one. Her parents had made it pretty clear she couldn't have one until she was a sophomore. But she was the only student in her entire high school without a phone. Her friends had to call her on her mom's phone. And forget about texting. It was more than embarrassing. It was pathetic.

Beep! Beep! Tanner pulled into the driveway.

Melissa gulped down another bite of pancake.

"Thanks, guys, you're the best—really, the best." Melissa shook her head. "That's Tanner. Gotta go."

"You barely ate anything," Mom protested.

Melissa stooped over and shoveled in two more bites as she threw her backpack over her shoulder.

"Happy birthday, sweetie," said Dad.

"Happy birthday," Mom echoed.

/ / /

Kick, kick, fan. Kick, kick, kick, down—into the splits.

Melissa's heart thundered in her chest. The last chord of the band echoed throughout the stadium, hanging in the air for a moment. The note was then overpowered by applause from the bleachers.

Knee up, stand up, step right, cross. Bow, two, three and stand and smile.

She beamed toward the stadium lights. She had nailed the routine—every kick, turn, and step of it—the last halftime performance of the football season. Melissa ran toward the sidelines with the other members of the team. Adrenaline popped through her veins like fireworks. Metallic gold pompoms crinkled by her sides.

"Woo-hooo!" Alyssa, the captain, shouted.

Melissa turned to hug Lindsey. As she squeezed her friend's polyester uniform, she caught a glimpse of Beau running back onto the field. She could see only his dark eyes peeking out from his helmet, but she knew it was Beau by the number fourteen tattooed across his jersey.

Lindsey was saying something.

"Uh-huh." Melissa nodded as they released their hug.

Lindsey turned to see what was mesmerizing Melissa. "Who are you ogling?"

Melissa hadn't told anyone except Gracie about her crush on Beau. She had just met all of her other friends at the beginning of school, and she didn't want them to think she was silly. Beau would never like her. She just grinned.

"Tell me who it is!" Lindsey demanded, her voice rising in pitch.

Melissa looked around to make sure no one was listening.

"Promise you won't tell?" she asked, tilting her head toward Lindsey's.

"Promise." Lindsey nodded.

"Beau Pointreaux," Melissa whispered. She didn't

want anyone to know, especially Jill, who was walking by with permaglare on her face.

"Shut up!" Lindsey squealed. "That new guy? He is sooo cute! Does he know you like him?"

"Well, he didn't," Melissa said. "But I'm sure he does now, thanks to you."

Lindsey waved her hand. "He didn't hear. We have got to get him to ask you out." Lindsey giggled as they walked back to their spot in the end zone.

"There is definitely no chance of that." Melissa shook her head. Then she stole another glance at the sidelines. There he was—number fourteen. Her heart jumped in her chest like a piece of popcorn in a pan of sizzling oil.

Even though she was sweating from her performance, the chilly autumn evening made her shiver. She pulled on her navy and white wool letter jacket. She cheered and laughed and even watched a little bit of the game with the other girls. The Huskies were winning by six points as the clock ticked down the end of the season.

"Seven, six, five," the girls chanted.

"Four, three, two, one," the crowd joined in.

"Yea!" Lindsey and Melissa jumped up and down, cheering a victory.

Eventually the troupe headed back to the band room, where they changed out of their uniforms. As she pulled off her white boots Alyssa announced, "Anyone who's interested, we're headed to Pizzaro's to celebrate!"

"Sounds good to me." Lindsey licked her lips.

"I love their cheese sticks," Melissa said, imagining

the gooey, melted mozzarella. She pulled at the snap on her jeans. They felt snug. "But I should really head home. Mom and Dad are waiting for me, and I have piles of homework."

"C'mon." Lindsey cracked her gum. "I bet one of the older girls will give us a ride. You can ask your folks. Plus, who does homework on a Friday night?"

"Thanks. Next time." Melissa squeezed Lindsey, slung her bag over her shoulder, and waved to some of the other girls as she made her way out the door. Football season may be over, but basketball season was just starting. The dance team would still have practice on Monday.

She walked down the narrow hall lined with navy blue lockers toward the parking lot. She could almost smell the tangy, greasy air that lingered in the pizza parlor. She wanted those cheese sticks. But if she was trying out for captain, she knew she would have to slim down.

"Hey." A thick voice, sounding like a Southern drawl stirred into a New York accent, caught Melissa off guard.

Beau stood near the large metal doors leading to the parking lot. His hair was wet, and his soap smell was stronger than ever.

Melissa felt her body tense like she had been tapped in a game of freeze tag. Then a goofy giggle gurgled from her throat.

"Hi." Melissa cocked her head. "You startled me. The game was great, really. I loved watching us win."

Why couldn't she think of anything clever to say? Beau was so cute and was actually talking to her, and she was just rambling.

"Thanks." Beau seemed so calm and mellow. The way the dimple showed in his left cheek when he smiled made Melissa feel dizzy. "You headed out?"

"Yeah, you? I thought all the players probably went out or something."

There was an awkward pause. Melissa heard her heart beating. She had to say something so Beau wouldn't hear it too. "I mean, some of the squad is going out, but, well, I wasn't in the mood, and I have to spend all weekend studying. Did you study French yet?"

Great. Now she sounded like a dork—studying on a Friday night.

Beau opened the heavy door for her.

Melissa's left index fingernail popped up to her mouth. She pulled it out. *No chewing!*

Before she knew it, they were in the parking lot. She could see her parents' silver van.

"No, I haven't studied for the test yet," Beau answered. "Do you want to get together Sunday afternoon and look over it?"

"Yeah . . . yeah, that would be great." Did he just suggest they get together? Probably just because she was good at French. He just wanted to study with the nerd to do well on the test.

"Do you want to come over to my house? Or I could come to your house?" Beau asked.

"You could come to my house. I mean, I'll have to check with my folks, but I'm sure it will be fine." Melissa nodded.

"I'll call around noon to check, okay?"

Melissa felt all fidgety inside and didn't know if she could stand there alone with him much longer.

"Super!" she said. Then with a grin, she added, "Bye!" and flipped her ponytail. She wanted to hide inside her parents' van where she didn't have to think about what to say or what he thought, but she also wanted to stand near him smelling him and listening to his accent forever.

Melissa paused in the middle of the parking lot, widened her eyes, and shook her head. She could see Beau walking toward a black Jeep.

Beau turned and waved. "Happy birthday, Melissa."

How did he know?

Chapter Five

Melissa plopped down in a blue plastic chair and put her tray on the round table where her friends were already eating.

"A salad!" Raven shrieked, tilting her head. Her café au lait skin was accented by beautiful deep brown eyes and a heart-shaped mouth with lips so naturally pink she looked as if she were wearing lipstick. Raven's glossy black hair was always perfectly in place in a hip 1960s flip. "What's up with that?"

"I'm just trying to be healthy," Melissa muttered, looking down.

"Healthy, shmealthy," Lindsey chanted, popping a French fry in her mouth. Lindsey could eat buckets of fries and get away with it. She was so tiny.

"How'd you do on the test?"

Melissa looked up and saw Beau standing beside their table. He looked especially handsome in a black shirt that set off his dark hair and eyes.

"I did okay, I think. I mean, I'm sure I screwed up that essay, but hey, whatever. I think I aced the vocab, thanks to you." Melissa grinned.

"Vous êtes une étudiante extraordinaire!" Beau winked and walked away, carrying his tray. His French sounded so exotic in the cafeteria.

Melissa's cheeks felt like freshly lit candles. He had made a point of coming over to talk to her, even when her friends surrounded her. It broke some barrier or code or unwritten school social rule.

As soon as he was three feet away, the table erupted in giggles.

"You have to tell us all about it!" Emma begged, dipping nachos in bright orange goo. Melissa adored Emma and envied her fiery red hair, but seeing Emma eat the epitome of junk food only to constantly complain about her weight made Melissa nauseous. She wanted to toss Emma's plastic nacho bowl into the trash for her.

Emma and Lindsey were best friends from grade school. But Melissa wasn't quite sure if Emma liked her or not. She seemed so different from sweet beauty-queen Lindsey. Theirs was just one of the four grade schools that fed into Spring Hill High. Raven moved here from Atlanta and played soccer with Gracie on the girls' junior varsity squad. At the beginning of the school year, the girls had clung together, and the five of them had become inseparable.

"Yeah. We want details," Gracie added.

Melissa swirled the iceberg lettuce with her plastic fork. "Well, he came over on Sunday, and we studied French. No big deal." She coyly shrugged.

"That's huge!" Raven exclaimed.

"And your mom went for that?" choked Emma, scrunching her freckled nose.

"I didn't know if she would at first, but his mom dropped him off and came in and introduced herself. That helped a ton." Melissa ate a cherry tomato. Its juice squirted the inside of her mouth. "She had on this cross necklace, and our moms started talking about churches in the area for the Pointreauxs to join, and that scored big points. How could Mom not like a churchy family?"

"So how long did he stay?" Gracie asked.

"Three hours!" Melissa's eyes widened and her ponytail bobbed behind her. She remembered how quickly the afternoon had gone, how she felt so comfortable and nervous at the same time with Beau next to her.

"Shut up!" squealed Emma. "You studied together the whole time?"

"Well, at first . . ."

"Then what?" Raven leaned forward.

"Then Mom brought out birthday cake and ice cream left over from Friday."

"So he found out it was your birthday." Lindsey winked as she applied a fresh coat of raspberry lip gloss.

"Yeah."

"What is it, Yellow? You're thinking about something." Gracie knew her better than the others.

"Well, it was weird, kind of. He already knew it was my birthday."

Brrrrriiinng!

The girls cleared their food and wrappers at the

sound of the bell. Melissa tossed her half-eaten salad into the trashcan. It was so tasteless. At least she didn't have time to eat much of it, but now she was starving!

Her stomach growled. It sounded like a cowbell rattling inside her. Thankfully no one else seemed to hear with all of the commotion of changing classes. All one thousand students flooded the halls, shuffling from one classroom to their locker to their next classroom in the allotted seven minutes.

Melissa slid behind Beau in French class. He turned and smiled.

"Can I buy a Tootsie Pop?"

Dear God, please let him like me.

"Sure, what kind?" Melissa asked as she opened the big yellow box she lugged from class to class.

"What do you recommend?" Beau's long lashes shifted down to peek inside.

"Chocolate. Definitely chocolate." She raised her eyebrows. "I'm gonna have one too."

"Then I'll take one choc-o-lat," Beau said in a perfect French accent. He handed her a quarter as Monsieur Renauld stepped to the whiteboard.

Melissa handed him the lollipop and trembled when his hand touched hers. It was soft and warm.

"Would you want me to walk you home today?" Beau's dimple appeared.

"Bonjour!" Monsieur Renauld began.

"Bonjour!" the class echoed.

"Definitely!" Melissa nodded.

Beau turned around to face the front. Melissa doodled his name in her notebook, then scratched it out so no one would see. While Monsieur Renauld conjugated verbs, Melissa replayed the first two minutes of class over and over again in her mind—the warmth of his hand, the way he had asked, as if they had already discussed walking home together, how his deep voice pronounced "choc-o-lat."

She unwrapped her Tootsie Pop, then stopped. She peeked at the side of the box: sixty calories and zero fat grams.

If she didn't bite into it, the lollipop lasted a long time. She could eat three a day instead of lunch and still be way under on calories. Plus, no one would give her a hard time if they saw her eating candy.

Melissa was famished. She popped the sucker in her mouth.

Chapter Six

A few days later, Melissa slammed her books on the kitchen counter. "A C! How could Mr. Dougherty have given me a C?" Her insides felt shaky, like when her hand held the electric mixer too long.

She flipped through her Chemistry test again. She didn't agree with some of the tricky wording on a few true-or-false questions, and she'd floundered on one of the essays. But a C just didn't seem right. It wasn't fair. She had never gotten a C before in her life—on anything.

Melissa opened the pantry: chips, Twinkies, cheese crackers. "Translation: fat, fat, fat," she murmured. She couldn't bring herself to eat any of it. She turned and opened the fridge: leftover bacon, *grease*, a slice of cheesecake, *calories, lots of calories. But I want something sweet or maybe crunchy. I need something!*

She settled on a diet root beer and a small bowlful of dry Cap'n Crunch. She sipped the bubbly soda slowly, savoring the sweet Splenda-laden foam.

Melissa carried her snack to the kitchen table, where she thumbed through her Algebra book. She had a test over five chapters tomorrow. She hadn't been able to study before now because of her Chem test on Friday and the English paper she turned in this morning. Each chapter had twenty practice problems. She figured if she could plow through all one hundred problems she'd be ready. She looked at the clock, then back at her book. She tossed a handful of cereal in her mouth and started writing numbers.

She was finishing the last problem in the first chapter when the phone rang.

"Hello?"

"Hey, Melissa. It's Beau."

Like he had to tell her who it was. She'd recognize that drawl anywhere. Her heart fluttered.

"Hey, what's up?"

"Well, you know the Christmas dance is coming up in a few weeks, and, well, I was just wondering, would you go with me?"

"I would love to!" Her eyebrows almost reached her hairline.

"Great! Well, we can work out everything later. I just wanted to make sure no one else asked you first."

"I would have told them no," she blurted. How embarrassing—she couldn't act even a little bit cool.

She heard Beau laugh softly on the other end.

"So what are you doing?"

What is he *doing?* Melissa wondered. *Does he still have on that forest green long-sleeved polo with the collar that reaches his curls in the back? What is he eating for a snack?*

What does his house look like?

"Studying Algebra," she said with a moan.

"Me, too. Five chapters is outrageous!"

"Yeah, there're like a hundred practice problems, and maybe two of them are easy."

"Well, I wish we could study together, but this time you're on your own." Beau laughed again.

"I'll try to muddle through." Melissa caught herself gnawing on her fingernail.

"Okay. See ya tomorrow."

"Okay, bye." Melissa hung up the phone and spun around the kitchen.

How would she ever be able to concentrate on math?

She picked up the phone and dialed Gracie. Gracie's voicemail clicked on.

"Hi, it's Melissa. Gray, guess who asked me to the Sugar Plum Stomp? Call me!"

Melissa munched the last few crumbs from her bowl. She started to walk back toward the pantry.

No.

Last weekend she and Gracie had seen the perfect dress at the mall. She had even tried it on and imagined herself dancing with Beau. Even though she had just met him, she had hoped Beau would ask her but hadn't wanted to get her hopes up too high. Now she could buy the dress. But she'd need to lose at least five pounds to look really good in it.

She did twenty-five jumping jacks right there in the middle of the kitchen. Her arms slapping on her legs reminded her of the new sequence she'd learned yesterday at practice.

And slap, two, three, four, turn around—she rolled her head in perfect tempo—and box step, three, four . . . Melissa stood there. She couldn't remember what came next. She tried again.

And slap, two, three, four, turn around, box step, three, four. Nothing. Her mind was blank. How was she going to be picked for an officer if she couldn't even remember the routine?

Her neck felt hot and prickly. Her shoulders stiffened. *Calm down*, Melissa told herself.

She picked up the phone again and punched the buttons.

After the beep she exhaled and said in a flurry, "Hi, it's Melissa. Linds, I'm trying to remember that new step from practice and have completely spaced out. Please call me before it drives me insane."

"Okay. Okay," Melissa scolded herself aloud. "I need to study. This test is tomorrow, and I need an A."

Melissa sat back down and picked up her pencil. Her fingers trembled as she tried to set up the next problem.

She put down her pencil and opened the pantry. She was reaching for the box of Twinkies when the door opened.

"Hey, Mel," said Mom. "Caught you with your hand in the cookie jar?"

Melissa flushed and drew back her empty hand. "Just looking." Her voice cracked as she said it. "Can't decide what I want."

"Well, how about pizza tonight to give you some fuel for studying? I know you've got another big test tomorrow." Mom walked behind Melissa and gave her a peck on the cheek.

Melissa tensed at the word *test*, not softening to Mom's kiss. She was so angry about her Chemistry test. She didn't want Mom to know she'd gotten a C. She didn't want Mom to hug her and feel how flabby her tummy was. Mom wouldn't want to order pizza for her then. She obviously already thought Melissa ate too much, busting her in the Twinkie box and all.

"Melissa, are you okay?" Mom asked.

God, what is wrong with me?

"I'm fine. Fine!" She nodded and smiled. "Beau asked me to the Sugar Plum Stomp. I'm just kind of dazed. You know?"

"Really? That's great! He seems like such a nice young man." Mom put her purse on the counter. "I liked his mom, too."

Melissa pulled another root beer from the fridge.

"We *really* need pizza now. We need to celebrate!" Mom winked and picked up the phone. "I'll call Pie in the Sky and put our order in. By the time it gets here, you can allow yourself a study break."

"Thanks, Mom." Melissa sat back down. Before Mom could pick up the phone it rang.

Melissa flinched. What if Beau was calling to cancel? She swung around and knocked over her root beer.

"Dang it!" she blurted. Her whole body shook as she went to the counter to get a wad of paper towels.

"Mel, are you okay?" Mom asked as brown bubbles flooded the table. "Hello?" She listened and then nodded. "It's Lindsey. She says she can't talk because she's grounded from her phone, but the step is kick-ball-change."

"Thanks," Melissa answered, wiping up the soda and shaking her head. "Kick-ball-change. Of course, that's it."

/ / /

$\mathcal{M}$elissa's eyes burned and itched when she finally climbed the stairs. She had done it. She had completed all of the practice problems and reworked her way through the ones she'd missed. Her pointer and middle fingers stung from gripping a pencil for that long. Her parents' room was already dark.

Melissa rushed her way through her bedtime routine. She held her toothbrush to her mouth and stopped. She'd better weigh herself before she brushed. The toothpaste calories might make a difference. She stepped on the scale and twisted her mouth. She wanted to lose five pounds—no, maybe seven—before the dance! Melissa patted her tummy. She had already lost two since she started her salad routine over the weekend. Just five more. She could do that.

She popped on her pj's, crawled under her thick yellow comforter, and turned on her bedside lamp. Her leather-bound Bible sat on the nightstand waiting for her. They had a nightly date.

The words on the delicate page blurred. She struggled to keep her stinging eyes open. She forced herself to read the words, although they didn't register in her sleepy brain. She closed the heavy book and returned it to its spot, clicked off the light, and grabbed her tattered blankie she had kept since she was a baby. Its softness comforted her. She and Beau dancing across the gymnasium floor waltzed through her dreams.

Chapter Seven

*M*elissa spent the next six weeks planning the night of the dance with her friends. They strategized the perfect dates, selected the most fantastic dresses, and mapped out the details of the evening.

A lot of the kids were going out to dinner before the dance. Melissa knew her parents would never go for an unchaperoned event with boys. She didn't think most of her friends' folks would approve either, so the girls had devised a plan. They prepared a fondue feast for their dates at Emma's house. Some of the parents were there to chaperone and to chauffeur them to the dance. The girls had a blast picking the menu, shopping for groceries, and preparing the food.

"You look beautiful, my lady." Beau bowed as Melissa opened Emma's front door. He looked so handsome in a suit. His crisp white dress shirt contrasted smartly with his dark features. His red-and-white-striped tie looked like a candy cane. It was perfect for the Sugar Plum Stomp.

Melissa had spent the whole day primping. She had painted her fingers and toes with nail polish, Poinsettia

Pleasures, the exact same shade of red as her dress. She had curled her poker straight hair in delicate ringlets, then piled the curls on top of her head like she'd seen in a *Brides* magazine. She'd even given herself a facial!

Now she twirled self-consciously in her red satin dress. Some of her friends wore more elaborate gowns, but Melissa stuck with the one she had originally seen with Gracie. She felt as glamorous as a movie star but sucked in her belly, feeling the slick satin against her skin. She had only lost eight of the ten pounds she had eventually decided to lose, and as a result the dress felt tight. Between handfuls of buttered popcorn while watching movies with Beau and the fudge sprinkled with crushed candy canes she and Mom had made for Dad's office Christmas party, she had cheated on her diet a few times. She didn't want anyone to notice she was watching her weight.

"Stop showing off, Yellow. There is soooo much to do," Emma whined. Emma's red hair flounced against the back of her strapless emerald green dress as she stomped back into the kitchen in her heels.

"I'll help," Beau said, tilting his head toward the kitchen.

"No way." Melissa smiled. "Dinner's supposed to be a surprise. The other guys are in the family room. Want a soda?"

Melissa put her hand on the small of Beau's back and nudged him away from the kitchen. The thick fabric of his suit felt warm to her chilly hand.

"Sure." Beau peeked into the kitchen. "That surprise sure smells tasty."

Melissa went to the fridge, grabbed a Coke, and took it out to Beau.

"Yo, Yellow," Emma barked. "Remember you came in here to help!"

"Sorry, sweetie. I'm just getting Beau a drink. I'll be right back."

Melissa passed Gracie on the way to the family room. Her lavender tulle dress flattered her petite frame and golden skin.

"Did Emma yell at you, too?" Gracie whispered so close Melissa could smell the sweetness of her jasmine perfume.

Melissa nodded, hoping Emma couldn't hear them.

"Either it's that time of the month, or she and her date are not getting along." Gracie winked.

Melissa winked back and stole into the safety of the family room. If it was Emma's time of the month, Melissa was secretly envious. Not that she enjoyed getting her period. It was messy and inconvenient, but it was normal. She had missed her last period, and that was not normal. She'd read articles stating athletes and super-skinny girls were often irregular. She didn't feel skinny, but she rationalized that dance team counted as a sport, making her an athlete. At least she tried to convince herself that dance was the culprit. But Melissa still felt uneasy about the whole thing. It was such a personal topic. She didn't feel comfortable talking about it with her friends, not even Gracie. They'd all think she was crazy.

When the food was ready, the girls called in their dates, and everyone gathered around the table. Old jazz tunes sung by Billie Holiday played from the speakers. Emma clanged her fork against her crystal goblet filled with sparkling cider.

Ting ting ting.

"There's a little game we're going to play with our dinner, which as you can see is fondue," Emma bellowed, waving a fondue fork like a magic wand. "For those of you who haven't fondued, you spear a piece of bread or fruit on the end of your fork and dip it in the cheese—or a piece of steak or chicken into the hot oil." Her fork pointed to the avocado green pot bubbling with Swiss cheese and the white ceramic pot full of sizzling oil.

"If your food falls in the pot, you have to trade seats with the person to your left. Got it?"

Everyone laughed and nodded.

Beau leaned toward Melissa. "Keep your food on your fork, darlin'. I want to stay close to you all night."

Melissa flushed. "We'll see," she answered and stabbed a cube of apple on the tines of her fork. She successfully swirled it in the Swiss and savored the tangy cheese clinging to the green apple, slowly chewing the tiny morsel.

Emma lost her piece of steak on the first try. As more and more people put their forks in the pots, more and more food fell. People forgot whose fork was whose.

Melissa was relieved by all of the seat switching and fork mix-ups. It took the pressure off her, knowing no one was watching what she ate. She lost track of how many times she changed chairs, but she knew exactly how many bites of fruit and bread she consumed. After a lot of laughing and teasing, in the end there were only a few strawberry stems and crumbs of bread left on random plates around the table.

"There's no more food," Raven announced. "It must be time to boogie!"

/ / /

Melissa gasped as she and Beau entered the school gymnasium hand in hand. It was completely transformed. With the pastel tulle covering the walls and the strands of tinsel dangling from the ceiling, the gym looked like the Land of Sweets straight from *The Nutcracker*. Melissa almost expected to see the Sugar Plum Fairy flitting across the floor.

A twang of electric guitars came from enormous speakers that the DJ had set up by one of the basketball hoops. A punch and cookie station sat at the other end of the room. Everything twinkled with white swirling lights reflected from a revolving mirrored ball hanging from the middle of the ceiling.

The air felt warm and heavy and smelled like the perfume counter at a department store. After Melissa, her friends, and their dates drank glasses of sweet, fruity punch and danced to a couple of popular songs, a familiar beat boomed through the speakers.

"Our song!" Lindsey and Melissa squealed together.

The music to one of their dance team routines was playing. The squad all ran to the middle of the dance floor. Lindsey grabbed Melissa and dragged her to their places in line. Melissa stepped and turned, trying to execute the routine the best she could without getting tangled in her dress and heels. Everything went okay until they got to the high kick sequence. Melissa's legs were trapped in her dress, and J. T., who stood next to her, toppled over, pulling Melissa with her.

Lindsey laughed. Alyssa doubled over, giggling. Melissa burst out laughing too. Soon the whole team was hugging and hooting. It seemed the entire school was clapping for them.

Melissa half-walked, half-tumbled back toward Beau.

He high-fived her. "Great job! I never get to see you perform, you know. I'm always in the locker room at halftime."

"Sorry that was the performance you saw." She laughed. "I, of course, always get to see you play."

"Not fair!" He tweaked her nose. "Let's grab some more punch."

The lights dimmed, and Frank Sinatra's voice crooned "The Way You Look Tonight" over the speakers.

"Shall we dance?" Beau extended his hand.

Melissa felt dizzy. The sound of horns booming from the speakers tickled her ears. She put her hand in his as they glided toward the dance floor. His hand felt so warm. It made her skin tingle.

"You look really pretty," Beau whispered as he spun her beneath his arm.

Melissa never felt pretty, but for a second she believed him.

The whole night swirled and twirled for Melissa. She couldn't believe it when the harsh fluorescent lights turned on and the music turned off. Melissa felt like she was going to explode with excitement while Mrs. Pointreaux drove the few short blocks to Melissa's house.

Beau got out of the Jeep and walked her to the front door. He reached for Melissa's hand and gently kissed her knuckles. There was that tingling again.

"I had a great time, my lady."

"Me, too," she said, beaming.

Then, for an instant, Beau's lips softly touched hers. She closed her eyes and tried to memorize the moment— the strength of his arms around her, the clean smell of soap that was so distinctly Beau, the scratchy wool of his suit against her bare arms. The kiss seemed to last both one hour and one second all at the same time.

Beau pulled back. Melissa opened her eyes. Silver flecks like the lights cast from the mirrored balls at the dance floated in front of her.

"Melissa, remember when we were talking about you getting to watch me at the games, but me not getting to see you?"

"Sure." Melissa tilted her head.

"Well, I thought . . . if you want . . ." He paused. Then Beau reached inside his coat. "I thought if you wore this on your jacket, then we could sort of be together at the games, and all the time. Would you?" He held out the gold football-shaped pin that he wore on the white S of his letter jacket. Melissa parted her lips but couldn't eke out a sound.

"I'm sorry." Beau shook his head and curled his fingers over the pin. "I didn't mean to push you. Good night," he whispered and turned.

"Wwwwait," Melissa finally squeaked. Beau turned back toward her.

She reached out her hand. "I'd like that. I'd like that a lot."

"Really?" Beau smiled and placed the metal pin in her hand.

"Really." Melissa beamed.

"Good night, for real then." Beau kissed her lightly on the cheek.

She forced her lips to part and her tongue to move until the two words "Good night" came out. As if watching a movie, she watched him walk down the driveway and back to his mom's Jeep.

Melissa felt like Cinderella as she climbed the stairs. She didn't want the evening to end. She thought of Beau's lips on hers, and the silver stars returned.

She put on her snuggly flannel pj's and opened her Bible. She knew exactly what chapter she would read tonight: Psalm 96.

Sing to the LORD a new song;

sing to the LORD, all the earth.

Sing to the LORD, praise his name;

proclaim his salvation day after day.

Dear God, thank You. Thank You for this night. Thank You for my friends, for the dance, for the chance to get dressed up like a movie star, and for making Beau like me. God, I am so happy. I know I couldn't be any happier than I am at this very moment. Thank You! Amen.

Chapter Eight

"Eighty-one, eighty-two." Melissa practiced holding her splits. Her inner-thigh muscles ached.

Ding-dong.

"Ahhhh!" she moaned, walking to the front door. "Hey." She smiled at Gracie and Lindsey.

"Hi. Whatcha doin'?" Lindsey asked, walking in with a brown paper grocery bag.

"Practicing my splits. I just got to eighty-two seconds. I'm trying for two minutes."

"Better you than me." Lindsey smiled. Lindsey had no interest in trying out for captain, so there was no tension between the friends. Melissa was relieved she could be open with Lindsey and that she didn't have to worry about who was practicing more or who was better at which moves.

Gracie walked toward the kitchen. "This is going to be fun!"

Gracie and Lindsey started unloading their sack while Melissa pulled out bowls and pans. Monsieur Renauld was offering extra credit points for anyone who baked a *bûche de Noël*—the traditional French Christmas cake—and brought it to class. Lindsey had French with him right after Gracie and Melissa, so they decided to make it a group project.

"So I was wondering what you're doing about Christmas?" Lindsey asked, cracking eggs into a glass bowl.

"Oh, the usual." Melissa bent over and stretched out her right calf. "We'll go to church on Christmas Eve, then to my Nana and Papa's for a big family thing on Christmas morning."

"Not about that, silly. I mean, that's nice and all, but what are you doing about Beau and presents?"

"I'm getting Drew a sweater." Gracie smiled and spun around the kitchen. "He looks soooo good in sweaters. Not that anyone asked."

"Sorry, Gray," Lindsey said. "You two are just such old news, no offense."

"True love doesn't have to make headlines." Gracie smiled.

Melissa had wondered about this for days. She and Beau were boyfriend/girlfriend. The pin proved that. She wanted to get him something, but what?

"I don't know!" she anguished. "I want to get him something great, but I don't want to be the crazy too-into-him girl."

"Like, how about his-and-hers T-shirts?" Lindsey winked.

"Very funny." Melissa laughed.

"I know," Gracie said in a sly voice. "Some cologne?"

"No way! That is so cheesy! Plus, he already smells wonderful, like soap."

"Okay, how about something less mushy, like gift certificates for ice cream or pizza?" Gracie suggested while measuring flour. "Then he'll have to take you to those places."

"Always thinking of me, aren't you, Gray?" Melissa joked. She envisioned herself in the short-skirted captain's uniform. Then she imagined scooping spoonfuls of ice cream into her mouth until the uniform popped at the seams. "No," she said, shaking her head.

"Well, don't ever say we didn't try to help," Lindsey said with a snort. "Since I don't have a boyfriend, I have to live vicariously through the two of you."

"What happened to your sweet Sugar Plum date?" Melissa asked while stirring with a big wooden spoon.

"Brock had this annoying habit of popping his gum. It drove me crazy!"

Melissa laughed. "You're the one who's crazy!"

"Typical Lindsey," Gracie added. "Not liking a guy because of the way he chews gum!"

"Whatever." Lindsey shook her head. "Now how do we do this?"

Melissa read the directions from the back of their French book. "Bake cake for thirty minutes and allow to cool. Once cooled, spread cream filling evenly over cake. Starting with a short end, roll cake, jellyroll style, until completely rolled. Secure with toothpicks and frost." She rubbed a patch of flour off her eyebrow. "So let's put the cake in the oven and make the filling while it cooks."

"I get to lick the batter," taunted Lindsey.

"Me too!" Gracie chimed in.

Melissa couldn't bear the thought of all that sugar and butter, but she went along with it. "What about me?" she chimed in, sliding the tray into the oven.

She grabbed a spoon and scraped some remaining batter from the side of the bowl. She turned and placed her spoon toward her mouth, fake licking it while throwing an eggshell down the drain. While by the sink, she tossed her untouched spoon into a bowl of soapy water.

"So Mom said I could have a Christmas party. Nothing big, just yummy food and *The Grinch*. Maybe Elvis singing 'Blue Christmas' in the background." Melissa raised her eyebrows.

"I'm in!" Lindsey said, licking batter off the side of her mouth.

"Can I bring Drew?" Gracie asked, fluttering her eyelashes.

"Sure, as long as you promise to help."

"I promise." Gracie put her fingers up in a scout's honor.

"Me, too!" Lindsey squealed. "I love Elvis. I'll be so bloooo," she sang into her spoon as if it were a microphone.

Melissa whapped her with a dish towel, and they all laughed until tears poured down their faces.

After their cake was complete and her friends had left, Melissa scrubbed and scrubbed the dishes, trying to remove every last fattening drop from the glass and metal. She polished the metal pan until she could see her distorted reflection in it and scoured the glass bowls until they were as clear as crystal. While her hands were immersed in bubbles, she wondered what she was going to get Beau.

/ / /

*D*ecember 21 was Melissa's Christmas party. Gracie, Raven, Emma, and Lindsey all helped put it together. Melissa also invited some other girls from the dance team and some friends from the youth group at church. But the guest Melissa couldn't wait to see was Beau.

Together Gracie and Melissa decorated the family room with tiny twinkling white lights and red velvet ribbons. The Christmas tree and the porcelain nativity scene underneath the lowest boughs set the scene.

Lindsey and Emma baked a batch of Chex mix so big they had to use the turkey roaster to hold it all! Raven baked cookies shaped like wreaths, made brownies topped with red and green frosting, and cut up a platter of fresh veggies with fat-free ranch dressing as the dip. Melissa made bright red punch out of sugar-free cherry Kool-Aid and Diet Sprite.

Everyone sang Christmas carols, watched *How the Grinch Stole Christmas,* and snacked on holiday treats.

Melissa crunched on veggies and sipped saccharine-sweet punch to join in the fun with virtually zero calories. The crowd dwindled, but Beau stayed. After everyone else was gone, Beau pulled a package out of his coat pocket.

"Merry Christmas, Melissa."

"I have something for you, too. I didn't want to give it to you in front of everyone else, because . . . well, you know." Melissa blushed. "Just a sec."

She scurried upstairs and returned with the red package tied in a gauzy gold bow that she had hidden under her bed. "Merry Christmas."

"Should we open them?" Beau asked.

"You first." Melissa's heart beat as fast as a hummingbird's wings. What if he bought her something trivial, like a key chain? Or what if he bought her something way too expensive, like jewelry?

Beau's lips curled in to a grin as he lifted from his box the tickets to a Christian rock concert Melissa had finally decided to buy, despite it being two months away.

"I've heard these guys on the radio. They're pretty good." He looked at Melissa. "Thanks."

"You're welcome." She smiled.

"Now you." He motioned toward the package in her hands.

Melissa slowly ripped the glossy wrapping paper, not wanting to appear too anxious. Three CDs tumbled out: a homemade Christmas CD titled *Sugar Plum Songs*, the CD that had the song the dance team had danced to at the Stomp, and Frank Sinatra's *Greatest Hits*. A little card was taped around the spines of the discs.

To Melissa—I thought a dancer could never have enough music. Now you can't forget the time you danced with me. Beau

She beamed. "They're great! Thanks!" She leaned over and hugged him.

"Really? Good. Now"—Beau paused for dramatic effect—"I wonder who I'm going to take to this concert?"

Melissa turned scarlet.

/ / /

*M*elissa was filled with Christmas joy as she read her Bible that night. "But the angel said to them, 'Do not be afraid. I bring you good news of great joy that will be for all the people. Today in the town of David a Savior has been born to you; he is Christ the Lord" (Luke 2:10-11).

Dear God, Thank You for Christmas, my family, my party, my friends, and for Beau—especially for Beau. Amen.

Chapter Nine

Christmas vacation flew by. Melissa slept in, went to the movies with her girlfriends, hung out with her folks, and read books and a pile of magazines.

She even got to see Beau three times. Once they ice skated at the Ice Chalet. They held mitten-encased hands as they skated round and round the frozen rink for hours. Another day they bundled up in scarves, hats, and snow pants and sledded down the sloping hill behind Beau's house. They sipped rich hot cocoa afterward and giggled. They also met at the mall one afternoon to listen to their high school chorus perform Christmas carols. Melissa felt grasshoppers jumping in her belly when Beau draped his arm around her shoulders for all the choir and crowd to see.

Melissa also spent two hours every day practicing dance in her basement. She stretched, kicked, spotted, and snapped. She practiced old routines for precision. She made up new routines to her favorite songs. Officers were responsible for choreographing a lot of the dances, and she wanted to be prepared.

On January 4 school started again.

"Bonjour!"

"Bonjour, Monsieur Renauld!"

"I hope everyone had a *joyeux Noël*." The class broke into a din as everyone began sharing stories about Christmas break.

Monsieur Renauld continued, "But now it is time to get back to our studies. I was lenient first semester focusing solely on the French language. This semester we will also focus on French geography and French culture." His nasal accent lilted from his long, narrow nose.

Groans filled the room. Melissa opened her textbook and scanned the next chapter.

"Beau, will you pass out these handouts, *s'il vous plaît*? These are articles from a French newspaper. They include everything from movies to politics in Paris. You will receive a packet like this each week."

Beau handed Melissa a packet and rolled his eyes. She smiled at Beau, then grimaced when she looked at the packet. The articles were completely in French!

In Algebra, Mrs. Poppendeck announced she would start giving weekly quizzes to keep the students "up to speed on the plethora of new material they would be covering."

Raven waved to Melissa in the hall before Chemistry. "Hello, Yellow. How's the first day back?"

"Great! I mean, I so don't want to be here," Melissa said, "but I will get to see Beau every day."

"You are so twitterpated," Raven said.

"No. I'm not in love or anything. I'm way too young

for that." Melissa shook her head. Well, maybe this is what love would feel like when she was older.

"I know, I know," Raven drawled. "But he is super cute."

"Isn't he?" Melissa giggled. "Anyway, I'm not excited to see Monsieur Renauld every day. I swear he expects me to be fluent in French in just months!"

"I'm freaked out about History. How are we supposed to remember the names of all those dead guys?"

"Please don't even get me started on History!" Melissa raised her eyebrows. "How will I ever keep my grades up *and* be good enough for captain?"

"Smarty pants, you're the last person I'm worried about," Raven teased. "You always have the highest grades." Raven waved to one of her brother Randy's friends as they wove their way down the congested hall.

"Hardly! High school is so incredibly hard!" Melissa tugged on her brown mane to tighten her ponytail. Several strands of hair remained in her hand like coffee-colored wisps of cotton candy tangled in her fingers. She discreetly dropped them on the floor behind her, hoping nobody, especially Raven, had seen.

"You'll do fine. Gotta run to English. We're probably reading eighteen novels this week." Raven laughed.

"Later!" Melissa darted to the door of Chemistry. Down the hall she saw Beau, but he looked like he was in deep conversation with the basketball coach. Mr. Harris's mustache bobbed up and down as his lips moved. His dark eyes flashed with intensity. Melissa shrugged and decided to talk to Beau later.

At home Melissa pulled out her Chemistry book. She desperately needed to pull her grade up. She tried memorizing the semiconductors on her periodic chart. Blah, blah, blah. She couldn't concentrate. She slid the textbook back into her backpack. She picked up *501 French Verbs. Manger—to eat, je mange, tu manges, il/elle mange, nous mangeons, vous mangez, ils/elles mangent.* "Got it," Melissa said, sliding the book back into her bag.

"Speaking of eating, I'm hungry." Melissa was getting used to the permanent pit in her stomach, but sometimes it felt emptier than others. She turned toward the kitchen, then saw her yoga mat rolled up by the basement door. "I shouldn't be eating. I should be working out."

She took her mat down the stairs and flopped on the squishy blue foam, extending her legs, and pointing her toes in front of her. She leaned over until her nose touched her knees, feeling the satisfying pull on the underside of her thighs and the insides of her calves. She'd better do some sit-ups.

"Mel," Mom called from the kitchen.

"I'm down here."

"Can you come up a minute?"

"Yeah," Melissa answered, dreading going into the kitchen. How could she keep from snacking if she was surrounded by food?

"Are you in the mood for spaghetti or lasagna for

dinner? I'm cooking Italian. I just can't decide what."

As Melissa topped the stairs, she saw Mom's back, peeking in the pantry.

"Lasagna!" Melissa said without thinking. It was one of her favorites.

"If I make it, will you help?"

"Sure, anything for your hot, cheesy lasagna, Mom." But as soon as she spoke the words, Melissa regretted them. How could she subject herself to such a decadent meal?

/ / /

In bed that night Melissa felt uncomfortably full of spicy garlic bread and gooey pasta. She hadn't been able to resist! Her face was warm, and she felt nauseous from the guilt of her gluttony. She read in Paul's letter to the Corinthians that the human body is home to the Holy Spirit and that we should take care of it.

Dear God, I'm sorry I ate like a pig. I know my body is Your house and I should take care of it, not cram it with carbs. It was yummy, though. Is that bad? Is it awful to enjoy food so much? I think I shouldn't be so obsessed with food. It seems selfish. Let me know. Amen.

Chapter Ten

The shrill beeps of Melissa's alarm clock jerked her from her slumber. Red numbers declared it six o'clock in her dark room.

"Ugh!" She closed her heavy eyes for one second, then forced them open. This was the first Saturday of training sessions with Todd for officer tryouts. She had to be in the gym ready to dance in one hour, but she didn't feel like she could move. She pulled back her warm covers. The chilly morning air bit her skin.

Melissa shivered. The hot spray from the shower prickled then finally permeated her goose bumps. She let the heat sink in, waking and warming her.

After pulling her soft gray sweat pants and matching hoodie over her shorts and T-shirt, she headed downstairs. She knew she should eat something to give her enough energy to get through practice, but she also knew Todd would never pick a fat girl to be captain!

Melissa rooted through the bread drawer. Blueberry bagels—perfect. She toasted half a bagel and pulled a banana from the fruit basket sitting on the counter. She took the cream cheese out of the fridge and read the label: 10 grams of fat per two tablespoon serving.

"Wow! I don't need that." She decided to just eat a dry bagel.

"Good morning." Dad ruffled her hair on the way to the coffeepot. "Early for a weekend, don't you think?"

"Morning, Dad." Melissa sat down at the table. "Rehearsal for officer tryouts. Did Mom tell you?"

"Oh yeah." He rummaged through the cupboard for a filter. "I'm really proud of you for doing this. You never know until you try. Right?"

"Right."

Melissa took a bite of bagel and told herself it was just as yummy this way as with cream cheese and so much healthier without it.

"Did you see Mom before she left?" Dad asked.

The rich scent of coffee permeated the kitchen.

"No, she must have left before I came down." Melissa washed down the dry crumbs with a glass of orange juice.

"Well, maybe you'll run into her at the church. She's setting up that pancake breakfast thing there."

"Maybe, but I usually go in the back door, straight to the gym. I've gotta run, Dad. See you later."

"Yeah, I'm on deadline, but I'll be writing from the house. Guess we're all up way too early for the weekend. Come see me when you get home. I'll look forward to the break."

At 6:40, Melissa was out the door.

The frigid January wind undid all of the warming of

her shower, but it also roused Melissa's senses. She huddled inside her coat as she tromped to the church gym. Even in January the high school gym was booked with boys' and girls' basketball, wrestling, and cheerleading.

Five other girls from the team were already there— four juniors and one sophomore. Melissa was the only freshman. She smiled at her teammates as she unbundled herself. She mentally sized up their abilities. Katie and Julia were sweet girls and good dancers but not very organized or dedicated. They were usually late to practice or forgot their props. J. T. was the most together person she knew and an excellent dancer, but she was quiet. The captain would need to be more assertive. But Stacey. Well, Stacey . . . she had it all! Stacey's crystal blue eyes didn't notice Melissa watching her. She was too busy stretching her ever-tan, muscular legs.

And then there was Jill. Jill sat on a bench completely relaxed. Her clumpy mascara seemed smeared in the early morning. Or was it left over from last night? Melissa tried to like everybody, especially the other girls on the team. But with Jill, it wasn't so easy.

"What are you doing here?" Jill glared.

Melissa smiled and shrugged, wondering why she *was* here. She was only a freshman. What was she thinking? She glanced at the clock: 6:55. She watched the minute hand tick, hoping no one else would show up. She tried to shrink her limbs into her baggy T-shirt like a turtle hiding in its shell.

"Okay, ladies, are we ready to rumba?" Todd's voice filled the gym as he came in the side door wearing faded black sweatpants and an equally faded navy blue sweatshirt. He clapped his hands as he moved front and center.

All six girls stopped what they were doing and gravitated toward Todd.

"Good morning! Isn't it?" He cocked his head and winked, knowing it was early and cold. "This morning is the first day of officer tryouts."

Tryouts! Melissa's inner voice screamed.

"I thought this was practice for tryouts, Todd," Katie blurted.

"Yes, yes. I did say that." Todd smirked and turned his back on them as he popped on the music. He turned back around.

"Today we will begin learning the sequence for officer tryouts. But . . . but, but, but there is a lot more to being an officer than performing the routine at the audition in March. I will begin evaluating all of that other stuff"—he waved his hands inwardly together—"starting now."

Melissa exhaled. *As long as actual tryouts aren't today!* Still, her heart vibrated in her chest as if she'd just done thirty high kicks. Todd would be watching how they learned, how they acted toward one another, what their attitudes were. She rolled her shoulders back, stood up straight, and smiled. She couldn't control the other girls, but Melissa could take charge of how she performed. *I will smile. I will be alert. I will pay attention. I will ask the right questions. I will act like a captain.*

"So how many of you braved it here?" Todd asked. "One, two, three, four, five, and six. Not bad, that's almost half of our returning ladies. Let's get started."

Boom! Boom! Boom! The music pulsated.

"I love this song!" Melissa blurted. Her eyes popped open in surprise at herself.

"You would." Jill snickered.

Melissa felt the heat of embarrassment burning behind her ears.

Todd smiled and squeezed Melissa's hand as he circled by. "Me too!"

Melissa didn't dare look at Jill but could feel her rolling her raccoon eyes.

"And five and six and follow me." Todd tapped the waxed wood floor with his left foot. Todd demonstrated the first sequence while the girls tried to follow his movements.

"Now, again!" Todd shouted, shuffling and spinning.

"Your turn." Todd started the music again.

"Pow!" emphasized Todd.

Melissa shot her right arm up toward the ceiling and her left hand straight in front of her. Both were in perfect jazz hands, and her chin snapped upward. She was staring right into the bottom of the basketball hoop. *Was Beau at basketball practice right now? He must be practicing a lot. He hasn't called in days. Is it just basketball?*

Slap, slap. The sounds of hands hitting thighs and dancers changing positions echoed through the gym.

"Melissa, care to join in?" asked Todd.

Melissa felt the searing heat spread from the nape of her neck, up her scalp, and around her ears. Hot tears stung the corners of her eyes, but she fought them back. She spun around to face the back wall and joined in the kick sequence two steps behind the others. She forced a fake grin and concentrated on the routine. This was not the time to wallow in her mistake. It would only draw more attention to her. Todd always said, "If you mess up, act like you didn't, and the audience will never notice."

Two hours later Todd finally announced, "That's a wrap." Melissa's legs fumbled to the bleachers and collapsed. She sucked down half her water in one gulp and wiped her sweaty forehead with the fuzzy towel she had packed in her bag.

"You look winded," Jill sneered as she zipped her jacket.

"What a fun routine." Stacey bobbed her head from side to side as if still dancing.

"It is fun," Melissa agreed. She was thinking to herself, *Fun but really tough*, but she didn't want the other girls to think she was incapable.

Julia grabbed her bag as she headed for the door. "Oh so fun and so very easy." She overemphasized her words, tossed her head back, and laughed at her sarcasm.

"Ha, ha, very funny," answered J. T.

Melissa popped her earbuds in and pushed play, hoping her fallback band, the Beatles, would drown out her uneasiness. She walked home as quickly as she could, her hood pulled up against the chill.

She was such a fool! She couldn't even concentrate on the routine. She had to think about Beau. He probably wasn't missing shots at basketball thinking about her! The heat of embarrassment returned, spreading all the way across Melissa's forehead.

Jill was awful! How could she be so mean? Melissa's eyebrows felt like someone was pushing them. Her jaw was stiff. Why was she getting so worked up? Why was she even doing this? She would never make captain! She should have slept in!

Jill's sneer flashed in her mind. At that moment, Melissa slipped on a patch of ice and fell on her knees, ripping a hole in the knee of her worn pants. Her iPod crashed to the ground, yanking the earbuds from her ears, where they got tangled in the confines of her hood. The notes of *Rubber Soul* bounced on the ice and dissolved in a pile of snow.

A sharp stinging throbbed from her knee. The icy pavement bit her crouched legs with cold. The street was empty. She let the tears spill down her face this time. There was no one to see them.

Dear God, are You telling me I shouldn't try out? I'm such a mess! I'm awful at Chemistry, Beau hasn't called, and I'm a big clumsy cow! Are You punishing me? What have I done? What could I do better?

Melissa untangled the wires from around her head, retrieved her iPod, and wiped it clean on her pants. She stowed the whole contraption in her bag, stood up, and started for home. Melissa stopped at the flashing "Don't Walk" at the crosswalk. Her tears felt like icicles on her face. She drew her wool letter jacket tighter to chase off the chill. Her tears halted as she felt Beau's football pin poke her mitten. She wore it on her dance team letter.

Thinking of Beau's warm hand placing the cold pin in hers made her smile. She inhaled the crisp January air.

Please help me do my best, God. Please.

Melissa stopped herself. She knew she shouldn't ask God to let her be captain, but it was what she wanted. She lifted her hand to her mouth to nibble her nails but only found wool mittens. She sighed.

Please help me do the best I can. I'll do whatever You want. I'll be less greedy about junk food. I'll study harder. I'll practice more. Please? Amen.

Chapter Eleven

Brrring. Brrring.

Melissa jumped from the warm indentation on the couch where she had been watching her favorite show. The rest of her family remained glued to the TV as she darted into the kitchen practically out of breath. She smiled, cocking her head sideways so her ponytail flopped. The number on the caller ID was not Beau's.

"Hello?" Melissa straightened her head and closed her grin.

"Hello, Melissa, it's Mrs. Gregory. Is your mom there?"

"Yeah. Just a minute, Mrs. Gregory." She sulked back to the family room.

"Mom, phone."

"Thanks, sweetie." Mom took the phone from her hand and smiled.

Melissa's stomach felt hollow like the inside of a chocolate bunny. The corners of her eyes stung. Why wasn't it Beau? She slunk back into her seat, curled her legs up to her chest, and tucked them under her hooded sweatshirt.

Ever since school had started back up, things hadn't felt right with Beau. Sure, homework was overwhelming. She had Saturday morning officer rehearsals on top of regular dance team practice. He was busy with basketball. But Melissa hadn't seen Beau outside of French and Algebra classes in two weeks. He hadn't called either. What had she done wrong?

She reached for a handful of the popcorn Dad had popped. Melissa hoped to fill her empty feeling.

No, she told herself. *I won't eat it. I can't make Beau call me, but I can make myself look good. Beau would like me more if I were thin. Todd will think I'd make a better captain. I can control what I eat. I told God I would.* She retracted her hand.

Dad chuckled his deep laugh along with the canned laughter on the TV. Melissa looked up. He was smiling at her. She smiled back as if she also thought the show was funny. She wished Beau was sitting here smiling at her. She missed him.

Should she call Beau? Melissa shook her head. He hadn't called her, but she hadn't called him either. There was something about calling boys. She had never done it. She wouldn't let herself start now. Mom was on the phone anyway. Maybe when Mom got off . . .

Ten minutes later Dad stood up. "Good episode. It's always so funny." Melissa felt a tug on her ponytail as Dad left the room.

"Dad!" He'd been pulling her ponytails as long as she could remember.

Melissa stood, looked toward the ceiling, and nibbled on her index fingernail. She walked into the kitchen. She tilted her head and wiggled her fingers. She was thinking about calling Beau. She rocked back and forth from her toes to her heels. Her shoulders relaxed when she heard Mom.

"I think we're supposed to be there by ten thirty so we can get places set and drinks poured before they open the shelter for lunch."

If Mom was still on the phone then Melissa couldn't call Beau. She exhaled. One less thing to worry about.

"Okay," she muttered to herself, "I have to read those crazy French articles and do all those Algebra problems before I can go to bed." She grabbed her backpack from the laundry room and unzipped it. "And write a poem for English!" she yelled at herself. "Aaagh!"

Mom covered the mouthpiece on the phone. "You okay, Mel?"

"Yeah. If you call having thirty-eight hours of homework to do okay. No, really, I'm fine. Totally fine." She shrugged her shoulders, and trudged to her room.

She dropped her books on her desk and pulled out her pj's. "I might as well get comfortable," she said and sighed. As Melissa undressed, she looked in the mirror. Her stomach seemed to protrude more than normal. Her thighs jiggled like Jell-O when she moved. She pulled on her snuggly flannels with the kitten print as fast as she could. She liked the way their loose fit hid her body.

"I need to get skinny."

She went back down to the kitchen to get her usual study snack, but with the willpower of a monk she grabbed only a diet root beer and a glass of ice. A cool calm filled Melissa's veins. She felt more in control than she had in days. She set her music to play Beethoven, "thinking music," she always called it. She stacked her homework carefully in order of importance. She plowed through French, Algebra, and even wrote a decent poem. Things didn't have to be overwhelming. She just had to be in charge of them. She couldn't let homework and Beau and dance rule her. She stayed up late, but she got it all done. When she finally closed her eyes, sleep immediately took over her tired brain and empty body.

She woke up exhausted but ready for her new plan. She weighed herself before and after showering. She weighed more afterward, which sent her pulse racing like a food processor. "No," she said out loud. "I only weigh more now because of all this wet hair. From now on I will only weigh myself with dry hair."

Downstairs she moved methodically, toasting a blueberry bagel, skipping the cream cheese. She started to pour a glass of orange juice but, noticing the caloric content of an eight-ounce serving on the carton, stopped at half a glass. She filled the rest of the glass with filtered water from the fridge. Melissa pulled out a shiny silver teaspoon and stirred. The small spoon clanged against the glass four times. She sat down at the table and took small sips and bites, enjoying the sensible breakfast she had prepared.

"See, I can still eat and be healthy and be on time for school."

As she loaded her dishes in the dishwasher, Mom and Dad came down still in their robes.

"Good morning, Mel," Dad mumbled as he shuffled his slippers toward the coffeemaker.

"Good morning, sweetie." Mom softly kissed the top of her head.

Beep! Beep! Tanner's horn blared from the driveway.

"Good morning, good-bye." Melissa laughed as she buttoned her coat. "Have a great day!" She felt good—really good. As she walked toward Tanner's car humming in the driveway, she began strategizing how to get through the rest of her day.

1. She could get a sandwich and a banana at lunch. She would eat just half of the sandwich.

2. She would write down all of her homework assignments in one notebook, class by class, so she could gather all of the right books to take home from her locker and have a plan of attack after dinner.

3. She would stretch extra long after dance practice so she wouldn't pull any muscles. She couldn't afford to get hurt now, not with officer tryouts approaching.

Chapter Twelve

Melissa got an A on her French paper, a 94 on her Algebra test, and successfully executed her lab in Chemistry. She placed a red check mark in her notebook next to "Chem Lab," flipped the pen, slid the red plastic cap from the bottom, and replaced it firmly on the top. She slid the pen in the zippered pouch of her backpack, where she removed a green pen. She removed the lid, placed it on the bottom of the pen, and wrote, "Chem—Read Ch 18." Her stomach growled. A hollow thud hit from inside. She told herself it was okay. In fact, the feeling excited her a little. She was on track and in charge. She only had one more class until lunch, and then she could eat a piece of fruit and half a turkey and tomato sandwich. Maybe today she'd buy an apple. Her mouth watered at the thought of the juicy sweet-mixed-with-tart flavor of the fruit. She replaced the green pen's lid and zipped it safely in its home.

Rrrriinng.

"Class dismissed." Mr. Dougherty smiled from behind his thin moustache.

Melissa sucked in her stomach and strode out of the

room.

"Oops!" Running over her list of homework again in her head, she ran smack into someone. Tootsie Pops sounded like hailstones pelting pavement as they scattered across the tiled floor.

"Sorry," she pleaded without looking up as she dropped to her knees to salvage the suckers.

"That's all right," came the familiar drawl.

Beau. Melissa looked up. "Hey." Her throat felt thick. Goosebumps tickled her arms. Her methodical manner melted. She dropped her gaze to the floor, not able to look into his soft brown eyes.

"Let me help you, my lady," Beau said with a fake bow. "What's going on in that head that you don't even see me?"

"Sorry." Melissa smiled and tilted her head. Her ponytail swooshed to the side. "How could I have not seen you? I'm just trying to figure out how I'm going to get through all of this homework. Crazy."

"Me, too." Beau slid the last chocolate lollipop into the cardboard box. "Between basketball and school I haven't been able to breathe."

Melissa stood with him. "Yeah, at least it's Friday." She widened her eyes. Maybe he would ask her out. Maybe everything was okay after all. She had been immersed in officer tryouts and school. Beau could be just as busy.

"Melissa . . ." Beau waited until she looked him in the eyes. "I'm sorry I haven't called."

"It's okay. Really. I've been buried, ya know? Officer tryouts, that French project, the Algebra exam. It's been insane—good, but insane."

"Are you really trying out for officer?" Beau tapped her on the back.

She felt like she'd swallowed an entire egg still in its shell. Melissa hadn't meant to tell him. She could feel the pink creeping across her cheeks.

"Oh, it's nothing, really. I'm just doing it for fun. Underclassmen never make it. I just thought it would be great practice. You know? Then maybe next year or the year after I'd have a chance."

"I bet you could be captain." He grinned.

"Not likely." Melissa rolled her eyes.

"See you later." Beau winked and turned down the hall to his next class.

Melissa could not contain her smile. She floated the rest of the way to English, plopped into her chair, and grabbed a chocolate Tootsie Pop. She was pretty sure it was the one Beau had just touched. Before she realized what she was doing, she popped it in her mouth. She jumped and pulled the sucker from her lips. Then she reminded herself it was only sixty calories and no fat. Plus, Beau touched it. She pulled a quarter from her backpack and slid it in her candy envelope.

At lunch the gang assembled at their normal table.

Lindsey pulled up an orange plastic chair and wedged her way between Melissa and Gracie. "So, Mel, how many Tootsies have you sold?" Lindsey asked.

"Almost two boxes since we got back from break, including the ones I've eaten."

"You don't look like you've eaten any of them," Gracie said between sips of juice. "You look model thin."

"Hardly." Melissa shook her head.

"I'm serious," Gracie said.

This should have been a compliment, but Melissa sensed something other than praise in Gracie's voice.

"So do y'all want to sleep over at my house tonight after the game?" Raven asked, her enormous brown eyes darting around the table.

"For real?" shrieked Emma. "I'm in!"

"Me too." Melissa nodded. "If my folks let me."

"Of course they will." Gracie elbowed her. "Drew has an away hockey game, so I'm in. We'll all come!"

Raven smiled, her ultra-white teeth shining between her stained brick red lips. "Mom said we could order pizza and bake brownies and rent the new movie with Jennifer Lawrence."

"I love her," Emma mumbled with her mouth full of Cheetos.

"She is gorgeous," Lindsey agreed. "I think she needs to pluck her eyebrows though."

Melissa looked at Lindsey's perfectly groomed brow line. "Only you, Linds, would even notice."

"I just don't know how some of these movie stars get away with poor hygiene. If I had all that money, I'd get my teeth bleached and a spray-on tan."

"Maybe you should be a makeup artist," suggested

Gracie. "I never know which color is best for what."

"Yeah, I'm pretty much a lip gloss and mascara girl." Melissa shrugged.

Lindsey scrolled her phone to Pinterest to show Melissa and Gracie the new Fabulous Fuscia nail polish she wanted.

Melissa glanced at the inviting images, but her mind replayed her conversation with Beau in the hallway. He'd probably be the star of the game tonight. Did he say he would call her? She couldn't remember.

Chapter Thirteen

And twist, twist, grab the box, and twist, twist, turn around, and twist, twist, HOLD, two, three, four.

Melissa kicked her right leg in the air exactly one second after Jill next to her kicked her right leg, and then Stacey kicked her right leg exactly one second after Melissa did. The whole team landed in the splits in a beautiful ripple effect.

Cheers and whistles came from the bleachers as the dance team held their pose with their chins up high and perfect smiles plastered on their faces.

Tweet, tweet, tweet, tweet.

The captain blew her whistle.

Slap. Slap. Slap. Slap.

The dance team stood up together like soldiers, turned to face the basket, and marched out the side door, the heels of their saddle shoes slapping the gym floor.

With her chin still pointed upward, out of her peripheral vision Melissa could see the players gathering around the bench. Beau's dark curls contrasted sharply against the white uniforms, making him easy to spot. Careful not to stare or break stride, she continued marching until she was in the hallway. Once outside of the audience's view, she tossed back her head and laughed. Blood rushed through her veins like a tidal wave. Was it adrenaline from dancing or from seeing Beau?

Lindsey hugged her. "Whoo!"

Jill walked by, gave a distinctly fake yawn, and pulled out her cell phone.

"I'm starving! Let's get something to eat." Lindsey motioned to the concession stand.

Melissa glimpsed her reflection in the sparkling glass of the trophy case as they walked past. She looked distorted and wide. Lindsey looked tiny and shiny.

"I'll come," Melissa said, "but I'm saving room for pizza and brownies."

"Oh, yeah." Lindsey wiped sweat from her forehead with her hand. "Let's just get a soda and find everyone."

Melissa was riveted to the action on the court while her friends gossiped about whether Princess Kate was pregnant again or not and discussed what kinds of brownies were their favorite.

"The fudgier and gooier the better," Emma offered, "but they go straight to my thighs." She slapped her jeans where they pulled taught around the tops of her legs.

"Well, we're making them with chocolate chips and frosting." Raven licked her lips.

Beau made a three-pointer. Melissa shot to her feet and cheered. The rest of the girls stood and cheered too.

"Why are we clapping?" Gracie whispered in Melissa's ear.

"Beau scored," Melissa whispered back.

"What's with you two anyway?" Gracie asked as they sat back down.

"Nothing much. We've both been so busy with basketball and officer tryouts and school and everything. You know, he's great. He's really great. But, it's nothing. Ya know?" Melissa smiled.

"Yeah, I know how *nothing* it is!" Gracie shook her head and rolled her eyes. "We'll talk later."

After the game the girls walked across the parking lot to Raven's parents' van where Raven's brother, Randy, already waited.

"Mel, wait up," Beau called from behind.

Melissa turned around. Beau jogged toward her and stepped up on the concrete bike rack.

"Great game," she managed.

"Thanks."

She waited. Would he ask her out for tomorrow?

Beau lowered his head. "There's something I need to talk to you about."

Lindsey winked at Melissa.

"Let's head to the van, gals," Gracie chirped.

Raven led the way.

"Hey, ladies, want a lift?" Randy called from the van window.

"Don't take too long, lovebirds." Emma elbowed Beau on her way past.

"What's up?" Melissa's heart raced. She sensed something was wrong. She didn't want to hear what he was going to say yet at the same time was riveted to every Southern syllable that came out of his mouth.

"Like I said in the hall, I . . . I . . . I'm just sorry I haven't called. I really am." Beau ruffled his hair with his right hand. "I just have so much homework and Coach is on me all the time." He looked up from the metal rungs used to lock bikes and met her forced smile. "I really like you, Mel."

Something *was* wrong. Melissa felt a queer shiver like when she ate ice cream too fast.

"I really like you, too." She willed her hands to stay at her sides so she couldn't bite her nails.

"But, well, with basketball and having to make grades and everything . . . well, Mom and Dad think I shouldn't date right now." Beau spoke to the ground.

He meant date *her*. At least he could look her in the eyes. Melissa felt like someone was stabbing her heart. An ache deep and sharp hit her chest. She couldn't breathe.

Beep, beep.

Raven's van pulled up alongside them.

"Looks like you're wanted." Beau nodded toward the van.

"Yeah, a slumber party at Rave's." Melissa bit her lip to hold back tears.

"Sounds dangerous." Beau laughed a hollow laugh. "Have fun with your friends."

"Always." Melissa turned and yanked the van's door open. What she wanted to say but couldn't was, "I'd rather be with you." That was one of the things. But there were so many more.

Her throat burned. Her heart felt like a balloon ready to pop out of her chest. Her eyes ached as she strained not to cry. As she pulled the door shut, Beau waved from the parking lot. "Melissa, I'm sorry." His voice lingered as the door slammed.

How could he end it like that?

"What was that all about?" Gracie rested her French-manicured fingers on Melissa's thigh.

Melissa shook her head back and forth. She couldn't speak. The corners of her eyes boiled with tears.

"Gracie, pass me that CD," Emma boomed, reaching her arm in front of Melissa's face.

Tears slid silently. Melissa hoped it was dark enough in the backseat that no one could see. She was embarrassed. What would her friends think if they knew Beau had broken up with her? If she wasn't good enough for him, she probably wasn't good enough for them either. Squished on both sides by warm bodies and surrounded by the boom of her favorite companion, music, Melissa couldn't remember feeling more alone.

Chapter Fourteen

*M*elissa pushed her angst way down inside of her. She stomped on her pain and decided to live it up. She couldn't remember the last time she'd gotten crazy and pigged out with her friends. She wanted to ignore the pit in her stomach.

She gobbled handfuls of chocolate chips while baking brownies with her friends. She laughed at Gracie's story about how her brother, Tanner, had started shaving and had held the razor the wrong way. She scarfed down three pieces of Papa Paulo's pepperoni. Melissa couldn't remember being this famished. She had become so regimented with her diet that she ate what she was supposed to eat when she was supposed to eat it, according to her rules, without regard to hunger. But now she felt completely empty, like there wasn't enough food to fill her hollow void.

She jammed to the new One Republic song Raven had put on and gobbled four brownies still warm from the oven.

She was almost feeling normal again until she went to the bathroom. The girl she saw in the mirror was ugly.

She was hurt. She was sad. Maybe it was Beau's parents, but maybe this was his way of dumping her gently. Did he want his pin back? He hadn't asked for it. He hadn't exactly explained what he meant by "shouldn't date right now" either. They didn't actually go on lots of dates.

Melissa tried to think about something she was in control of—something good.

Dance team? Captain audition practices were a disaster. Jill was evil.

School? It was a drain. Her workload was overwhelming, and she still hadn't pulled up her Chemistry grade.

Why had she eaten so much? As if devouring a lot of junk was going to make her feel better. Now she only felt worse. Melissa touched her stomach. It seemed to expand like a loaf of bread dough set out to rise.

She wished she could get rid of all the disgusting feelings inside of her. She wanted to get rid of the stress and the uncertainty. She wanted to undo whatever had caused things to go wrong with Beau. She wanted to take back all of the pizza and brownies.

Before she knew what she was doing, Melissa kneeled on the fuzzy periwinkle bath mat in Raven's bathroom. She reached behind her and looped the end of her ponytail into her ponytail holder, creating a bun. She examined the index and middle fingers of her right hand as they formed a peace sign. Her fingernails, jagged from biting, scratched the back of her throat.

"Agh," she gasped, squeezing her eyes shut.

She couldn't stop now.

She jammed her fingers down her throat farther.

Cuugghkk! She coughed, expelling her fingers, which were hot and moist. She hoped her friends couldn't hear her, hoped the music was loud enough to drown this out.

Again, Melissa leaned over. This time a hot gush filled her throat, sweet and sour and acidic. She removed her fingers and peeked in the toilet. Not a lot, but at least she had gotten rid of something.

Her eyes watered.

Melissa leaned back, disappointed. She had hoped to feel more triumphant, more in control, but she couldn't even make herself puke very well.

Then a surge rose in her throat. This time she couldn't control the hot mucousy bile. It overflowed out of her mouth and through her nose like the baking soda mixture out of her volcano science experiment in third grade.

The gagging made her eyes water, and her mascara smeared down her cheeks. Her fingers were covered with thick brown goop. She inhaled. She had to clean herself up. No one could know what she had done.

Like a robot, Melissa stood and turned the left faucet knob on high. She grabbed a wad of toilet paper and blew the remaining goo from her nose. She squirted a silver dollar–size dollop of soap in her left palm and began to lather with the hot water. She scrubbed her hands and arms up to her elbows. Then she scrubbed her face, erasing all traces of tears and vomit.

God, please don't let them know. Please don't let my friends know what I just did. Please make them still like me. I need someone to like me.

She smelled her hands. They smelled like the piña colada soap Mrs. Mack stocked in all the soap dispensers. That smell always made her think of Raven. She loosened her hair and let it fall down on her shoulders. She took a deep breath. She was ready, but she was sure her breath smelled like vomit.

Melissa meandered past the kitchen counter, where she grabbed a stick of gum from her purse and popped it in her mouth. The sharp taste of artificial sweetener almost made her gag again, but she knew the mint would help overpower the scent of her sin.

"Yeah, what's wrong with her anyway?" Emma's voice stung Melissa's ears.

"Things did *not* look good with Beau," Lindsey said. "I think she needs eyeliner and maybe a fitted sweater. She needs to make him want her."

"Give her a break, guys." Gracie's words hung in the air as the girls sensed Melissa's return. The sudden hush from her friends affirmed the "her" they were talking about. She bit her lip and forced a smile.

"Lindsey, I was hoping you could give me one of your famous makeovers." Melissa winked, pretending she hadn't heard them. "I figured I needed to wash away the old me so you could create a beauty queen."

Lindsey squealed with delight and pulled out her makeup kit.

"I've been dying to, Yellow."

Melissa flopped down onto the couch and chomped her gum. "I'm all yours, Linds."

"Well, which one?" Lindsey squeaked, holding up two eyeliners.

"Oh, whatever, how about blue?"

"How daring of you, Melissa. You're normally a more conservative girl." Lindsey grinned giddily.

"Wow!" Emma said, dropping cross-legged on the floor next to them. "Melissa, you look totally like a vixen. You'll have to do me next, Linds. Can you make me a size eight?"

Raven came in with a bowl of popcorn.

"Who's ready for the movie?"

"Roll 'em!" Emma shouted.

Gracie leaned over to Melissa and whispered, "Are you okay, sweetie?"

Melissa couldn't mask her mood for Gracie. They'd known each other for too long. They'd learned how to ride bikes together and compared treasures from the tooth fairy. They bought their first training bras together and went away to church camp together, able to leave home for a week only because they had each other.

"It's Beau. I'll tell you later." Melissa squeezed Gracie's hand. Gracie was such a perfect friend, even if everyone else was talking behind her back. She didn't blame them. She hadn't been completely honest with them. Maybe if she confided in her friends they wouldn't think she was such a case. Maybe they could even help.

Maybe her life wasn't a disaster. She had Gracie, and the others cared enough to include her in everything.

Melissa managed a "Let's see it, Raven." See, she was okay. She had let Lindsey make her over. She would not eat any popcorn. She would laugh tonight, and tomorrow she'd have officer training. She would work out really hard to make up for any junk left inside.

Yeah, she was okay.

Chapter Fifteen

"Melissa, Melissa." Melissa felt like she was on a swing, swaying back and forth, back and forth. She wondered who was calling her.

She opened her eyes. The blurry outline of Mrs. Mack came into focus. Melissa sat up straight.

"Sorry to wake you, honey," Raven's mom whispered. "Your mom's here to take you to practice."

"Thanks." Melissa yawned, stretching her arms fully into the air. She knew she had to move. What kind of captain would be late?

She pulled herself up, trying hard not to disturb her slumbering friends. She quickly and quietly rolled up her sleeping bag, stuffed her pillow inside the straps, and headed up the basement stairs in the purple XXL T-shirt from her church retreat that hung down to her shins.

"Good morning, honey," Mom called from the kitchen.

Melissa walked over and gave her a peck. She dropped her bed bundle beside Mom, who sipped coffee out of an orange ceramic mug with Mrs. Mack.

"I'll be a minute, Mom. I just need to brush my teeth

and stuff." Melissa fought back another yawn.

"I'd let you use the upstairs bathroom, but Randy's asleep up there. Do you mind using the one in the hall?" Mrs. Mack asked.

"No problem."

Melissa pulled back her thick brown tresses into a ponytail. She scrubbed her face with soap and cold water and brushed her teeth. After putting on a thin coat of brown mascara, she dabbed on cherry-flavored lip gloss. The sweet taste made her tongue tingle. She pulled on her workout clothes and rushed out of the bathroom.

"Can I get you something to eat, sweetie?" Mrs. Mack asked from the counter.

"Sure," Melissa answered, pulling on her letter jacket. "Maybe a bagel and a banana, if you have it?"

"Well, I don't have a bagel, but I bought donuts this morning." She motioned toward the white box on the counter.

"Yummy," Melissa said and opened the cardboard lid. Inside glazed, chocolate-iced, and sugar-sprinkled donuts tempted her. A squirt of sour bile shot into her mouth. "I'll just grab one for the road." She could barely look as she grabbed a bagel-shaped glazed donut and wrapped it in a napkin. Her stomach flip-flopped. She was afraid she was going to throw up again.

"Thanks for everything, Mrs. Mack. I had a great time." Melissa hugged her hostess. "Tell Raven I'll call her later."

"Thanks, Nikki," Mom said. "Come on, Mel, we'd

better go."

Melissa planned on telling her mom about Beau in the car, but Mom started asking about who was at the slumber party and what they ate and what movie they watched and how late they stayed up. Before Melissa knew it they were at the church, and she was climbing out of the car.

"Have fun, sweetie," Mom called. "Make sure you eat your donut. You're going to need some energy."

"Thanks, Mom."

Melissa still felt groggy as she pushed the heavy metal bar to open the rear door leading into the gymnasium. Her eyes felt like they had cotton balls in them, fuzzy and light. She tossed the donut in the large trash barrel by the entrance.

Everyone at practice seemed lethargic. Todd wasn't even dressed for dancing. Instead he wore baggy jeans, a sweatshirt, and a black knit ski hat. He held a Styrofoam cup, stark white against his brown hands. He tapped the rhythm to the music for their routine with his gym shoe and called out the moves while sipping his steaming espresso.

"And turn, turn, turn, turn, jump, and snap."

Melissa turned and turned, hands up, hands down, now to the side. She saw a rainbow as the colors in the gym blurred together. White ovals rimmed in pink and blue blurred her vision.

SMACK!

Her head hit hard against the gym floor. She felt the

cold wood, but her forehead, nose, and chin felt hot, like they were melting into the floor.

"Melissa, are you okay?" Stacey rushed to her side.

Her face felt like it had been hit with a meat cleaver.

"Everyone stop!" Todd called. He ran to Melissa and rolled her onto her back. Bright lights flashed in her darkness. She scrunched her closed eyes tighter in pain.

"She forgot to spot," Jill jeered.

Melissa felt like a loser, falling flat on her face—literally. She might as well quit. She felt like she was eight years old. She just wanted to run to her mom's lap and bury her face in Mom's shoulder.

"Melissa?"

She opened her eyes to slits, and Todd wove into focus.

"I'm okay. Just clumsy," she mumbled.

He cradled her head in his surprisingly rough hands and helped her stand. She wobbled, then steadied.

"Sugar, did you eat anything this morning?" Todd asked sweetly.

She wanted to say yes. She couldn't let anybody know about her secret diet. Keeping it to herself was part of how she controlled it. No one could make her change what she ate if they didn't know how she was eating. But could she lie to Todd?

"A little," she mumbled.

"I was afraid y'all would do that. Ladies, gather around."

The team had already formed a group around Melissa.

"I know we're meeting early, but you need to eat a real breakfast before you come." Todd still steadied Melissa with one warm hand on her back and another on her bare arm. "I'm working you hard, and your bodies are tired. They need fuel. A car can't drive without gas, and y'all can't dance without food. Everyone got it?"

Everyone nodded and mumbled yeses.

"Okay, now who has something in her bag that Melissa can eat?"

"I do," said Katie. She bounded to her gym bag and back. "It's a granola bar. It's been in there awhile, so it may be a little mushed." She handed it to Melissa.

"Thanks." Melissa smiled.

"Now go sit on the bleachers and eat, girl. After the room quits spinning, you can join us." Todd nodded toward the bleachers. "J. T., give her a hand."

J. T. wrapped her freckled arm around Melissa's back. "Come on," she whispered. "You'll be okay."

As the music boomed and her teammates swirled and kicked in front of her, Melissa faced the granola bar. She knew she had to eat it. Todd was watching. She peeled the silver wrapper back to reveal the coagulated mass of oats and chocolate chips. It had more fat and calories than a plain blueberry bagel but less than a donut. She pulled a corner off and popped it in her mouth. It felt mealy. She struggled to chew. Around and around the gym went her friends and rivals. Around and around in her mouth went the same bite of granola bar.

When the bite finally dissolved, Melissa tried another bite, but that's all she could do. She still felt nauseous from last night. She stood up. Feeling more stable, she walked slowly toward the drinking fountain, testing her strength and stability. The cold water felt sharp and lively in her mouth.

Dear God, please help me do this. I have to be able to do this. I promise I'll do my best. I know I was stupid. I'm sorry I threw up. From now on I'll eat the right things in the first place. If I had just avoided all that junk food, it never would have happened. I know You have reasons for things. You must have a reason for Beau. I just don't know what it is. Please help me through this. I promise to be good. Amen.

Melissa found her place on the floor, thrust her arms upward, and leaned left. She made it through practice, but barely. Her moves were correct but not precise. She kicked when she was supposed to, but not as high as usual—not as high as Stacey. She pasted a smile on her face and kept moving.

Clap. Clap.

Todd signaled for their attention. "That's it . . . for today. See y'all Monday after school with the rest of the team." He took one last swig of his coffee and tossed the empty cup in the trash can. "Enjoy your day, ladies."

Melissa felt completely drained. She couldn't get out of the gym fast enough. Todd didn't make a big deal about her fainting, but she was sure all the girls would. They wouldn't mean it in a bad way. They would want to make sure she was okay and would want to know how it happened. They would want to make sure they wouldn't faint too. She couldn't stand the questions or the looks of pity in their eyes.

She dashed to the parking lot and exhaled in relief when she saw Mom waiting in the van. She opened the car door and plopped inside. Tears sprang from her eyes before she could buckle herself in.

"Melissa, what is it, honey?" Mom asked, placing her hand over Melissa's trembling one.

Melissa couldn't get a sentence out. "Practice . . . I was so crummy . . . and Beau . . . my friends." Sobs tangled her words.

"Hey, it's okay. It's going to be okay." Mom handed her a Kleenex.

Chapter Sixteen

*M*om turned at the black sign shaped like a coffee mug and pulled into the Morning Brew parking lot. "How about some cinnamon tea?"

Melissa felt so empty and cold. Tea sounded wonderful. Maybe it would warm her insides back to normal.

She nodded and managed a tiny grin. The grin allowed her to catch her breath enough to stop sobbing. She exaggeratedly inhaled through her nose and blew air out her mouth, puffing her cheeks.

Inside the coffee shop Mom opted for a cozy booth in the back. Melissa felt safe here, protected from the whirling madness that had become her life.

"Okay, kiddo." Mom looked serious. "You can run, but you can't hide. Time to tell Mom what's going on."

Melissa's eyes welled up again. She wrapped her fingers around her mug, allowing the warmth to seep into her hands. She closed her eyes. The scent of cinnamon filled her nose, and the spicy taste of tea tickled her tongue. She wanted to tell Mom everything, but she didn't dare.

"It's everything," she managed, still gripping her

teacup. "It's Beau. He broke up with me."

"Oh, honey!"

"It was stupid, really. Some blah, blah, blah about how much he liked me, blah, blah. I don't know." Melissa tucked some loose hairs behind her ears.

"Help me out." Mom's eyebrows slanted in. "Fill in the 'blah, blahs' so I can understand."

"I don't even get it, Mom. Plus, Valentine's is coming up, and we were supposed to go to that concert. You get the picture." The tickets. Now they wouldn't even go. Some Christmas present, and after all that deliberating! Melissa wondered if Beau would take someone else. More tears sprinkled her cheeks.

Mom sipped her tea, nodding.

"I know you really like him. Are you sure he doesn't still like you?"

Melissa nodded.

"What else, sweetie? You said your friends and dance aren't going well either."

"Well, I tripped over my own clumsy feet and fell flat at practice today. I am so not captain material. I guess I'm not supposed to be an officer, but it's okay. I mean, I still get to be on the squad next year, and being on the team takes less time than being an officer, so it's okay, really." She talked to her teacup, not daring to look into Mom's eyes.

"And my friends, they're really great. They really are. I mean, we had so much fun at Raven's last night. She's really sweet, and Lindsey's hilarious. She gave me a makeover. You should have seen me all goopy and curly." Melissa patted her hair and fluttered her eyelashes.

"Okay," Mom said, probing for more.

How did Mom always sense when she wasn't telling the whole story?

"I don't know. I just don't feel like I can talk to them about things. I mean, Gracie I can. She's the best. But the rest of them don't have boyfriends, and they just get all giddy about Beau and movie stars. They are so fun, really, but I have all this stuff inside of me, and they don't know me that well, and I don't want them to think . . ." She slurped her tea and didn't say anything more.

"You do have a best friend who will always listen to you and who will never laugh at you or judge you." Mom put down her cup on the wooden table.

Melissa knew Mom had good intentions, but there were still things she couldn't share with her. How could she explain to her own mother how her knees felt like pudding when Beau kissed her? Mom would absolutely freak if she knew about the dieting—especially the throwing up thing. Mom would probably send her into counseling. She was always talking about people who needed counselors!

"I know you'll always listen, Mom. Thanks." Melissa smiled.

"I don't mean me, honey. I'm always here, but some things are even hard to tell your mom. I mean Jesus.

He'll always understand."

Melissa knew that. She'd heard those words a thousand times. "Jesus is your friend. Jesus loves you." But she didn't think Jesus would be very happy with her purging or getting worked up over a boy. She drank some more tea. Her tummy growled so loudly it sounded like a blender on full speed. Her eyes widened with embarrassment.

"I thought all you girls did at slumber parties was eat!" Mom laughed. "I guess you didn't get enough. What would you like?"

Melissa ogled the glass case by the counter filled with decadent pastries oozing with jellies and creams. To the side she saw neatly stacked piles—bagels!

"A blueberry bagel would be great!" She was so excited to see her reliable standby. It was as if everything was going to be okay, simply because of a bagel in a neat stack.

/ / /

*O*nce home, Melissa used every ounce of energy to trudge upstairs to shower and get dressed for the day. She was exhausted! She pulled open her top drawer and saw the picture of Beau and her at the Sugar Plum Stomp in the Lucite frame she had paint-penned hearts on. Melissa turned it over so she couldn't see his face, then lifted it back up and kissed the smooth, flat surface. Her eyes stung. She laid the picture back down and shook her head, as if trying to shake Beau and the pain out of her heart.

Her spiral notebook sat on top of her dresser. She opened it and began to pen an hour-by-hour schedule for her day.

10:00–11:00: Shower, get dressed

11:00–12:00: Read French articles

12:00–1:00: Eat lunch—1/2 turkey and tomato sandwich, 1 apple, and water

1:00–2:00: Call Gracie and explain the Beau thing (If she's not home, call Lindsey or Raven to get scoop on what happened this morning after I left.)

Melissa planned each moment until bedtime and turned the page. The next page she titled "Sunday" in swirly letters and began a new schedule from waking to church to studying. Melissa felt more in control now. She had a plan. She looked at her clock: 10:18! She'd better get moving if she was going to be completely ready by eleven to read over her French.

French . . . Beau . . . French.

"No! I will not let him do this to me. I am good at French." Melissa's mind drifted to crowded cafés and couples throwing their heads back in laughter as she meandered to the shower.

Melissa made it through Saturday and Sunday. She plodded through each hour as she had planned it in her notebook, getting great satisfaction by checking off each activity as she completed it. She studied and practiced dance. She went to church and helped around the house. She felt as if she were in slow motion, but when she completed one activity, she knew exactly what to do next. This gave her little time to dwell on falling at rehearsal, throwing up at Raven's, or even Beau.

She picked at her food, but Mom must have equated that with the breakup and didn't even ask her to finish her veggies at dinner. Melissa had only cried twice since telling her mom.

The first was when she told Gracie the story about what Beau said in the parking lot. Gracie cancelled her plans with her boyfriend, Drew, and invited Melissa over Saturday night. They watched a silly movie that almost made Melissa forget. Almost.

The other time she cried was Sunday night before bed. Melissa climbed under her covers and turned out the light. She had been busy all day long, but then she was alone. There weren't any more things on her to-do list. There wasn't anything left to distract her. Even her Bible reading didn't console her. She couldn't find anything in the black print that applied to her. She sobbed and sobbed until her eyes couldn't make any more tears. She lay in the dark, shaking, until she fell asleep.

Chapter Seventeen

Melissa scuffled into her bathroom and hopped on the scale. She hopped back off onto the cold linoleum. The red digital numbers didn't display what she'd hoped after a weekend of starving herself. She turned on the shower to warm up the water and went to the bathroom. She squeezed toothpaste onto her toothbrush and lifted her brush to her teeth. "Wait!" she reminded herself. "I don't want to weigh in those toothpaste calories." She pulled off her pajamas and stepped back on the scale. She had lost two pounds in pee and pajamas.

"That's better." She took deep breaths. "But not good enough."

She wiped half the blue gel off her toothbrush before entering the shower. "Every little bit counts."

Melissa got ready for school. Her hands shook as she brought sips of watered-down orange juice to her lips. Her feet didn't seem to fit in her shoes. She couldn't get her backpack zipper on track.

She hoped she could do this. She would see Beau in French class for the first time since the breakup. Even if she made it through an hour of Monsieur Renauld without a breakdown, she was going to have to go to Algebra and see Beau for another hour.

She wore waterproof mascara, in case of tears, and her favorite soft yellow sweater for security. She had studied hard for both classes. Her plan was to participate and show Beau how smart she was. She hoped that annunciating with an authentic accent and solving involved equations would distract her enough to get her through. She hoped.

"Want an escort to French?" Gracie appeared by Melissa's locker as she was pulling *En Bonne Forme* from the top shelf.

Gracie joked and told stories as they walked through the crowded corridors. When they approached the doorway, Gracie reached out and squeezed Melissa's hand.

"You'll be fine, Yellow. You can do this. You are a beautiful, brilliant girl, not to mention my very best friend. Don't let him mess with you." Gracie's tiny fingers released hers, leaving a warm impression on her cold palm.

Melissa marched to her chair. She wouldn't look up or down or sideways, like a horse wearing blinders. She sat down, opened her notebook, moved her pen cap from the tip to the end, and immediately began writing her French vocabulary words for the week and their English counterparts in cursive.

Beau was there, of course, sitting directly in front of

her. She could see the shape of his shoulders and head, but she would not look up. When Monsieur Renauld began class, she stopped writing and turned her eyes to the left of Beau's head, gazing directly at her teacher.

She repeated French phrases, raised her hand, and answered several questions about the homework articles—all without looking at Beau. Melissa remained composed until she leaned forward to write the home-work assignment in her notebook. With her head closer to Beau, she caught a whiff of that perfect Beau smell. He smelled fresh-scrubbed, like laundry hanging outside to dry. A smile crossed her face, then she sat abruptly back.

Soap, of all things, would not lure her in.

She wrote the rest of her assignment with her body upright and her head erect.

Brriinnng!

Melissa pulled her fingernails out of her teeth, slid her books off her desk, and darted to the door before Beau could turn around. She wanted to wait for Gracie but couldn't risk facing Beau. She and Gracie could talk later.

She had done it. Her heart pounded under her sweater, and blood rushed so violently in her veins she actually felt her temples pulsing. She had gotten through an hour of being just inches away from Beau. So far, so good, but Melissa still had Algebra, and it was next. She didn't want to get to class before him because then when he got there he might try to talk to her. No, she had to arrive seconds before the bell rang, just like she had done in French. She snuck into the girls' bathroom to stall for time.

French had drained Melissa. She had forced her surroundings into a sort of haze, choosing only to hone in on her teacher and her notebook. It took a lot of effort to ignore someone's existence. She splashed shivering cold water from the sink on her face to energize her. She shook her head and splashed more water on her face until her skin tingled. Colors and sounds emerged from her cloudy surroundings. She put on a fresh coat of lip gloss and headed to class. Being late wouldn't be good either. She didn't want to draw attention to herself or get in trouble.

She opened her Algebra notebook and found a big smiley face signed by Gracie. Melissa cracked a grin. She survived Algebra just like French.

At lunch she hugged Gracie tightly.

"Thank you," she whispered as tears snuck into the corners of her eyes.

"For what?" Gracie smiled, hugging back. "I'm just your best friend and always will be."

Melissa pulled back before the tears spilled down. "Put it this way, you made my day. . . ." She couldn't speak for a second. "You made it okay, Gracie, really okay. And I really didn't think it could be. Thanks for the smiley."

Beau and his friends were coming. Melissa sensed his

presence from behind. She plopped in a seat and ducked her head, rummaging through her purse. She avoided his eyes once again.

Melissa peeled her orange and deliberately pulled it into pieces section by section. She broke pretzel twists into bite-size pieces and slowly crunched them, washing them down with bottled water. She listened to Gracie and Raven discuss soccer strategies, Emma bemoan her little brother, and Lindsey rate at least ten people who walked by on their shoe selections. She allowed the cocoon of her friends' laughter to surround her and protect her—at least for lunch.

Melissa managed the entire day of school without speaking to or having eye contact with Beau. At the end of seventh period, Melissa wanted to dash home and hide under her covers like a child in a thunderstorm, but she had dance practice.

The two hours whirled by with kicks and stomps and turns and splits. The music pulsed through Melissa's veins. The smile she pasted on her face almost became real. She was on today. She would not let her mind drift to anything, fearing it would drift to Beau. She remained focused on the routine and Todd's instructions. She pointed her toes and kept her fingers together. She snapped her head with precision and caught each beat perfectly.

/ / /

he next few weeks were almost identical. Melissa put all of her attention into her classes and dance, not allowing herself time to think about Beau. Yes, he was there. A shadow. A ghost always looming around a corner or in the desk in front of her, but she avoided him. She gave him no chances to talk to her, and she certainly wasn't going to speak to him. Her friends filled the gaps between classes. By the time Melissa got home from practice, she was so exhausted that all she could do was shower, nibble at dinner, do her homework, and collapse in bed.

Chapter Eighteen

On Thursday Melissa woke up, went to the bathroom, and stripped off her pajamas. She weighed in as she did each morning when she woke up and each evening before she went to bed. Her weight looked good today. She had lost the pounds she had planned to lose for the Sugar Plum Stomp, plus a couple more. She placed her hand on her belly and pinched a wad of skin.

"Not exactly tight," she moaned.

Melissa turned sideways in the mirror to view her profile. Her belly appeared to bulge. How could she still have a tummy? She gnawed on what was left of her nails. She'd need to lose that before officer tryouts. She was on the right track, though. Eating less, pushing herself harder at practice—it was working.

She squirted her favorite smelling lotion, Peach Cobbler, from its light orange bottle and bent over to slather it on her skin. She inhaled the sweet, sticky fragrance and pulled back.

"Oh my gosh! What am I doing? This can't be good for me! Anything called Peach Cobbler is bound to be bad, and here I am rubbing this creamy stuff directly on my skin." She scrubbed her hands in the sink, removing all traces of the lotion. "And look, number one ingredient: cocoa butter! Like I need to be putting cocoa or butter on me!"

Melissa closed the bottle and shoved it in the back of her cabinet. She wanted to throw it away, but since she had paid for it with her allowance she couldn't bear to pitch it. Her hands shook.

"Okay," she told herself. "Okay, okay," she repeated as she pulled on her clothes.

Melissa yanked three sections of hair, entwining one over another until a tight braid wove its way down her head. She grabbed her backpack and marched down the stairs.

She opened the fridge and pulled out the orange juice, pouring the usual half glass of water mixed with a half glass of juice. She opened the bread drawer and reached for the bagels. She didn't see them. Her pulse quickened.

They must be here.

Melissa pulled every item out of the bread drawer and placed it methodically on the counter: wheat bread, saltines, English muffins. No bagels.

"We must have some bagels somewhere," she said aloud.

She opened the fridge and the freezer. Blood rushed like a waterfall to her temples. Where were the bagels? She had to eat a bagel in the morning. It's what she did.

She rooted through the pantry and spun around too fast when she couldn't find what she was looking for. In haste, she knocked over her orange juice. The glass shattered on the tile floor. Splashes of pulp landed in patterns across the white surface.

"Mel, you okay?" Mom's sleepy voice mumbled from upstairs.

"Uh-huh," Melissa mumbled right before the sobs erupted. She sat on the floor next to her mess and shook.

Mom ran down the steps.

"Sweetie?" Mom looked at the floor and at Melissa. "Honey, it's okay. It's just a glass—an old one at that." Mom had a way of doing several things at once. She scooped up Melissa's fallen backpack, grabbed the rag hanging from the faucet, and began wiping up the spill. Next she gathered shards of jagged glass, stacking them neatly within the largest broken piece.

Melissa wanted to help but couldn't move. She was frozen with the uncertainty of what to do next. She had a plan to get her through this day. That plan included eating breakfast. Her breakfast meant a bagel. There weren't any bagels. What next? Should she eat something bad for her and feel guilty about the calories and fat? Should she skip breakfast and not have enough energy for practice? Could she even handle practice? Could she even handle seeing Beau again today?

Mom threw away the glittering fragments of green glass and wiped the remaining sticky spots on the floor. She sat down next to Melissa, who was no longer sobbing, just crying quietly.

"Mel, it's not about the glass, is it?"

Melissa shook her head.

"That stupid Beau!" Mom said, hugging her from the side. "Boys can be so awful . . . or so wonderful . . . or sometimes both."

Melissa nodded, still not composed enough to speak.

Mom handed her a Kleenex. "Let's splash some cold water on that beautiful face. He doesn't know what he's missing. And he is missing."

Mom scurried around the kitchen, pulled Melissa off the floor, and handed her a granola bar and an apple. "Take these. Tanner will be here any minute, and you'll need to eat something before school."

Melissa took the food and nodded.

She wanted to tell Mom it was more than Beau. It was Beau, for sure, but it was more. But she couldn't form the words, and she didn't want to cry again. She just stood there.

"You'll be okay, sweetie. I promise. I know it doesn't feel like it now, but you will get through this." Mom squeezed her.

Beep! Beep!

Saved by the beep, Melissa thought.

"Thanks, Mom," she managed to say and even curled her lips in the tiniest smile. "I'll see you after practice."

"Hang in there, Mel."

Melissa walked through the front door, thankful for the February wind whipping her face.

Chapter Nineteen

Melissa had been timing her entrances into French and Algebra so that she slid into her desk at the very last second, allowing no time even to catch Beau's eye. But today she arrived to Algebra early. She was still flustered by the bagel incident this morning, and her whole day seemed off because of it.

She sat in her desk and pulled out her notebook, deliberately going through her checklist for the day. She would not look up. She didn't want to see Beau when he came in the door. She didn't want to think about the shirt he was wearing or how fresh the scent of soap would be on his collar, but she couldn't push those thoughts from her head. She could actually smell his soap.

"Melissa," he whispered. Beau's hand lay flat on top of her shoulder. She shut her eyes tightly, then opened them.

"What?" she answered as coldly as she could, all the while feeling the warmth spreading from his hand and oozing over her shoulder like syrup dripping over a stack of pancakes.

"I've been trying to find a chance to explain to you. I didn't want to talk about this over the phone." His dark eyes drilled through her. "But you keep avoiding me."

"Am I?" she asked, shrugging innocently.

"You know you are. You slip into class at the last minute and leave almost before the bell rings. You haven't even looked at me in two weeks."

Brrriinng!

"Today, class, we'll be working on tangents." Mrs. Poppendeck's voice sounded foreign and out of place to Melissa. "Mr. Pointreaux, take your seat."

Melissa stared past Beau toward the teacher. Mrs. Poppendeck's hair was in a too tight perm. Her hooked nose reminded Melissa of the beak on a bird she had seen at the zoo. Mrs. Poppendeck's clothes looked like she had bought them fifteen years earlier, but she was thin—rail thin. Her shirts hung on her shoulder blades, and her ankles looked like cabinet knobs peeking out from under her longish polyester skirts. Melissa shook her head. How could her frumpy Algebra teacher be so thin? It wasn't fair!

Beau took his seat, glancing back at Melissa. She felt his eyes on her, but she didn't dare turn her gaze from Mrs. Poppendeck. She still heard his soft voice floating through her ears and still felt his fingers on her shoulder. Her stomach churned. Her neck burned. She worked on her middle nail, gnawing away the cuticle.

Algebra seemed to last four hours. Melissa never took her eyes from the chalkboard, yet she didn't hear a word

Mrs. Poppendeck said.

As welcome as the bell commencing class had been, the shrill bell signaling the end of class was five times as freeing. Melissa shot straight up and dashed toward the hallway. She gasped for air and bolted to Chemistry. She suffered through endless lectures in Chemistry and English. When English finally ended, Melissa ran without looking back to the girls' room, where she promptly made herself throw up. The tension she'd bottled inside for three hours exploded like soda out of a shaken-up can.

The same sweet sticky goo burned her throat as it had at Raven's. Her eyes watered. Her hands shook as she struggled to peel the wrapper off a piece of gum and pop it in her mouth. After mopping her face with thin, rough toilet paper, she emerged from the stall, splashed cold water on her face, and dusted powder on her nose. Melissa tried to look inconspicuous, like every other girl primping in front of the mirror.

"Mello Yello," Raven called from three mirrors down. "Great sweater!"

"Thanks." Melissa smiled while popping her mascara wand back into its pink plastic bottle.

"I'm starving," Raven said, hooking her arm into Melissa's. "Let's hurry so we can get in the front of the lunch line."

Melissa chomped furiously on her gum, hoping Raven wouldn't smell vomit on her breath. She listened to Raven rattle on about her crush on Jeremy and if she should send him a valentine, and if she did if she should send it anonymously.

They walked through the line. Crowded bodies pressed them, moving the two girls forward. Melissa ordered a cheeseburger and grabbed a banana, too. The smells of all the greasy foods swirled together and clung to the walls. Her stomach churned like a food processor blade. She already wanted to make another trip to the girls' room but couldn't with Raven standing beside her.

"Not hungry?" Gracie asked at their table as Melissa picked at her bun.

"No." Melissa shook her head. "It's Beau." She could barely say his name without tears springing to her eyes.

"The jerk," Gracie whispered, wrapping her arm over Melissa's shoulders.

"Guys are just so like that!" Lindsey said between mouthfuls of chips.

Melissa felt like she was digging around in the bottom of a candy bag hoping to find at least one last M&M. Even a brown one would do. But when she searched inside of her, she felt nothing.

At practice Melissa still felt hollow as she tossed her canary yellow nylon gym bag on the bleachers. She stretched her legs, trying to override the anxiety from her brain with the pull in her muscles. Her mind flashed to Beau and her Chemistry test tomorrow and the inch of flab she had grabbed around her middle this morning.

"Don't let Mr. New Orleans keep you down," Lindsey said, dropping her blonde head to her thin legs to stretch beside Melissa.

"I'm okay, really," Melissa said. "It's just so confusing. Anyway, I've got you guys, right?" She forced a smile.

"Always and forever." From her shiny lips, Lindsey blew a kiss.

Melissa wondered if that was true. Would her friends always be there for her?

Clap, clap, clap.

"Listen up, ladies, I'm tired, I'm cranky, and I'm going to work your tails off today. Okay?" Todd batted his dark eyelashes.

Melissa and Lindsey moved into line with the other girls facing the back of the gym. The music started, and one by one the dance team members snapped into poses facing front. On the third set of eight, they all clapped their hands above their heads, shouted, "Go!" and ran to their next formation.

"Good!" Todd called. "So good, in fact, let's see it again so that it'll freeze in y'all's pretty brains."

The music blared again. Over and over the girls ran to their places and jerked their bodies to the beat. Sweat dripped down Melissa's face. Electricity ran through her veins like the music pulsing from the speakers.

"And stomp, stomp!" shouted Todd.

The sound of stomping sneakers echoed through the gym.

"Turn, turn, and wig-gle." Todd walked around the gym, observing the girls from all sides.

Silver flecks, like fairy dust, danced in front of Melissa's eyes. She turned and slapped. The flecks followed her.

"And in and out and in and out." Todd's foot tapped the rhythm.

Melissa kicked, but she felt like she was spinning. The music lost its beat and sounded like a roar.

"And stag leeeeap!" Todd stretched out the word to fill the space in the music.

Melissa jumped and popped her hands, one up high and one to the side. The flecks took over until the silver swarmed into black.

Thud!

"Stacey, get the music!" Todd barked, trotting to the spot on the floor where Melissa had gone down.

Melissa heard Todd talking to her. She heard girls whispering.

"Is she okay?"

"What happened?"

"Did anybody see?"

Her eyelids pressed down as if they were taped shut. Melissa didn't want to open them. It was so much easier to lie still. She didn't want to face them—all the thin, bright-eyed dancers who were staring at her. She didn't want to take her Chem test tomorrow or explain all of this to her parents or face Beau in class yet another day. If only she could keep her eyes closed.

"Melissa, girl." Todd shook her gently. "Melissa, girl, time to get up."

Melissa lay there, the cold, hard floor enveloping her body. She squeezed her eyes tighter.

"You won't get away with that," Todd scolded. She could smell his spicy deodorant activated by his sweat. He placed his warm hand behind her back and lifted her to sitting.

"I'm okay," Melissa blurted, suddenly aware of her error. She realized how urgent it was for her to get up and dance. This was the second time she'd passed out at practice. Captains don't pass out.

"Everyone take five, except you, Lindsey," Todd called out. "Girls, get a drink, stretch those legs, rest up. I'm not done with you yet."

Melissa smiled as she leaned to stand. Todd gently pushed her back to sitting.

"I don't know what's up, Mel. But you've fainted twice in two weeks. Skipping breakfast might have done it the first time, but there's more to it. You're one of my best dancers. I need you the rest of the season and the next couple of seasons too." His face was only inches from hers, so she couldn't dodge his stern gaze.

"I'm fine, really. I promise I'll take it easy tonight after practice." Melissa nodded.

"Practice is over for you, honey. And I can't let you perform tomorrow night."

A cold, clammy sweat oozed from Melissa's pores, like garlic through a press. This couldn't be happening! She scrunched her eyebrows and shook her head so vehemently her ponytail slapped her face.

"It's not a punishment, Melissa. It's just reality. You need to take care of you. You need to see a doctor. What if there's something to all of this?" Todd turned to Lindsey. "Call her mom, Linds. You know the number?"

"Sure!" Lindsey trotted to her gym bag to retrieve her cell phone.

Todd stood and extended his hand. "Let me know what the doc says, and then we can put you back in."

"What about Saturday morning?" Melissa croaked.

"See the doctor, then we'll talk." Todd squeezed her hand and motioned her toward the bleachers.

"Okay, girls. That's more rest than you deserve. Now let's see if you remember what we worked on." Todd flicked on the music, and the team, minus Melissa, went to their places. Lindsey ran over to Melissa.

"Your mom's on the way." She gave Melissa a kiss on the cheek and ran to join the squad.

Melissa now felt like that empty M&M'S bag crumpled into the bottom of a stinky garbage can.

Chapter Twenty

"Are you okay, honey?" Instead of waiting in the car like usual, Mom came trotting to the side door of the church with her arms stretched out toward Melissa. Melissa flashed back to falling off the jungle gym on her first day at preschool and Mom running toward her. As much as Melissa wanted to turn into her mom's arms and have her problems go away with a kiss and a Band-Aid, she was also embarrassed by Mom's gushing emotion.

She fell down. She was fine. Period. Well, she wasn't completely fine, but what was she going to say? Melissa climbed into the car.

"Lindsey said Todd wants you to see a doctor." Mom bit her top lip but kept her gaze straight ahead, maneuvering out of the parking lot. "What's going on, Mel? How long haven't you been feeling well?"

Melissa wasn't sure which was worse, riding home with Mom or being banished from practice by Todd. She didn't have the words to explain to Mom *what* was going on. She didn't know *how long* it had been going on. Was it when Beau broke up with her? Was it before? Was it him or the eating or her grades? Was it captain tryouts or trying to act to her friends like none of it really mattered when all of it really did matter? It mattered a lot.

"It's nothing, really. I just fell, whatever," Melissa started to choke out, but instead of more words, sobs started from somewhere in her hollow stomach, racked her rib cage, and poured uncontrollably from her mouth and eyes.

"It's okay, sweetie." Mom took Melissa's hand in hers. "Whatever it is, it's going to be okay."

Once home, Melissa bolted to her room, turned on her music, and buried herself in pillows. She cried and cried until she didn't have the energy to cry anymore. Glancing at the clock, she realized she was usually still in practice at this time. She definitely didn't feel like studying. She wasn't ready to face Mom. She wasn't sure if she would ever be ready for that. She felt splotchy and smeary and achy all over. Her cheeks stung from the saltwater of her tears. Her eyes burned from her melted mascara.

She nibbled on her ring finger's nail, stood up, and changed the music from melancholy Rickie Lee Jones to melodic Sting, then meandered into the bathroom. She moved slowly, as if someone had pushed the frame-by-frame button on a remote control. Melissa turned on the shower. All of the thoughts swirling around her head disappeared in the soothing heat. The beads of water washed away her overwhelming sadness, leaving her numb. She felt like a robot drying off and dressing in fleece sweats. Melissa plopped on her bed and looked at her clock again. She had no direction, no purpose.

Picking up a magazine and flipping through a few pages, her gaze went right through the words and pictures. She put the magazine back next to her Bible.

"Of course," Melissa whispered. She picked up the heavy book. The smooth leather cover felt familiar and comforting in her hands. She flipped to the index and slid her finger up and down the topics until she found *food.* She turned to one of the passages.

> At his gate was laid a beggar named Lazarus, covered with sores and longing to eat what fell from the rich man's table. Even the dogs came and licked his sores.
>
> The time came when the beggar died and the angels carried him to Abraham's side. The rich man also died and was buried. In hell, where he was in torment, he looked up and saw Abraham far away, with Lazarus by his side. So he called to him, "Father Abraham, have pity on me and send Lazarus to dip the tip of his finger in water and cool my tongue, because I am in agony in this fire."
>
> But Abraham replied, "Son, remember that in your lifetime you received your good things, while Lazarus received bad things, but now he is comforted here and you are in agony." (Luke 16:20-25)

Melissa hastily grabbed the pen with purple ink from her nightstand and wrote in her journal:

> The rich man in Jesus' story lives in eternal anguish after eating rich feasts, but the poor starving Lazarus, longing for even scraps, goes to heaven. This must say something about pigging out on cake and popcorn. God wants me to eat meekly, so I can be meek. Right?

Melissa scribbled, finally feeling like she had heard an answer from God. She was so relieved to find Scripture that compared people who ate a lot to those who didn't. She was so worked up in what she thought the Bible said, she didn't take time to finish reading the passage. She knew she should pray about this, to make sure God was leading her to His conclusions instead of hers, but she knew what she wanted it to say.

Knock knock.

"May I come in?" Mom called softly from the door.

"Yeah." Melissa looked up.

"Sorry to interrupt, sweetie. I'm glad to see you writing in your journal. It helps to sort through your feelings."

Melissa nodded. She didn't want to sort through those feelings with Mom.

Mom waited, as if she hoped Melissa would divulge what she was writing. She had no intentions of sharing. "Well, dinner's ready. Did you want to come down, or should I bring you up a tray?" Mom offered.

Melissa couldn't possibly eat.

"I'm really not hungry."

Mom nodded. "Okay. I'll put a plate for you in the fridge in case you change your mind later. We're having tacos—with guacamole!" Mom grinned, rubbed Melissa on the back, and when she got no response, slowly left the room.

"Guacamole is, like, so loaded in fat!" Melissa said under her breath.

Melissa switched music again. The Beatles were perfect. Paul and John belted their hearts out about love and heartbreak, politics and nonsense, and her toes tapped and her heart ached right along with them. She painted her nails Pink Pizzazz. She organized her drawers, carefully folding every pair of underwear and matching the wayward socks that had been floating around the bottom of her drawer for months.

Around eight o'clock there was another knock at her door.

"Pumpkin?" It was Dad.

"Yeah," Melissa answered lazily.

Dad poked his head in the door to find Melissa surrounded by a pile of jeans and sweaters that she had emptied from their homes. He raised his eyebrows.

"Wow! I barely saw you there with all those clothes."

Melissa smiled.

"I snuck you up some fried ice cream. Mom went all out on her Mexican theme."

Melissa peeked in the bowl and saw a round ball of

cinnamon crunch. The honey topping smelled sickeningly sweet. Her stomach contracted.

"It's awesome," Dad said. "Warning, though, you need to eat it fast or that hot shell melts all of the ice cream inside."

"I'll proceed with caution," Melissa said in a low voice, then gave him a mock salute.

"I know you're not ready now"—Dad gently cupped her chin in his hand—"but tomorrow we'll need to talk about what's going on."

Melissa's eyes shifted to her carpet.

"There's definitely something wrong, sweetie. Cleaning your room is not normal behavior for a teenager."

Melissa laughed at Dad's attempt at humor. "Okay. I'm a closet cleanaholic. I've been hiding it from you guys, but now I'll come clean." She winked.

Dad smiled. "Cute. Seriously, Mel. In the morning, okay?"

"Okay," she said and nodded.

When he closed the door, Melissa took the bowl, waited a few minutes, snuck into the bathroom, and rinsed the ice cream down the drain.

Chapter Twenty-One

Beeep beeeep beeeep beeeep.

Like on every other school morning, Melissa's alarm went off. Like on every other school morning, she went to the bathroom, turned on the shower to heat up the water, weighed herself, brushed her teeth, showered, got dressed, and applied lip gloss and a layer of brown mascara.

She clunked down the stairs in her saddle shoes, her uniform skirt brushing her thighs.

Yesterday seemed like a fog. Melissa half-wondered if it had been a dream. She hadn't eaten dinner, hadn't even opened her backpack to do the homework that was due today, and had even fallen asleep with her lights on! She thrived on being organized and following the plan and the rules. Had she really let last night happen?

She tried to step lightly into the kitchen. The fluorescent lights surprised her. Mom and Dad sat at the table in their robes.

Melissa jerked back, tripped, and landed on the floor. A sharp pain sprang from her bottom.

She nervously laughed at herself. "You guys surprised

me," she said, pulling herself from the ground. "What are you doing up?"

"Remember, we were going to talk this morning," Dad said softly.

He had said that, but she had hoped he hadn't meant it or that he wouldn't remember.

"Why don't I get you some breakfast? You go ahead and sit down." Mom nodded toward Melissa's place, where a glass of orange juice already sat. Melissa assumed it wasn't diluted with water. She would only be able to drink half the glass.

"Tanner will be here in, like, five minutes." Melissa's voice shook and her eyes darted from side to side.

"I called him last night," Dad explained. "He's not coming."

"Okay."

Melissa sat down, not sure if her parents were letting her be late to school or if they were driving her and hoped to talk on the way.

"And I called school this morning." Mom brought over a plate piled with bagels to the table. "I told them you're not coming."

Melissa looked at her mom and back at her dad. These were the people who didn't let her miss school unless she had a fever or was throwing up.

"We have things to take care of that are even more important than school." Dad put his hand on Melissa's. "Your hand is freezing. Are you okay?"

"Yeah, just a little chilly this morning." She pulled

her sweater tighter around her uniform.

"Eat a warm bagel, honey. I'll make some hot chocolate. You get warmed up and filled up and relax. Dad and I will talk first."

Melissa nodded. She put half a bagel on her plate. It did feel warm. She took a bite. It tasted so rich and smooth, even better than normal. She ate another bite and another, then noticed little yellow drips on her plate. "Butter!" she squealed in dismay.

"Don't you like your bagels buttered?" Mom asked.

Melissa instinctively spit out the half-chewed piece of bagel that was still in her mouth. She wanted to spit out the other bites that were already somewhere down her throat. In her mind, butter was poison. It was fat. It was actually called fat.

Tears slid down her face as she gagged. She wiped her tongue clean with her napkin. The thin paper shredded on her wet tongue. She grabbed her juice to wash down the butter and paper remnants but remembered her drink was full strength, thus full of calories. She put her glass down in frustration. She felt totally out of control. She wanted to run, but Mom and Dad were now both really staring at her. There was nowhere to go.

Mom pulled her from her chair and hugged her tight.

"My goodness, Melissa. There's nothing left of you under that sweater!"

Dad put down his coffee and joined in the hug. Melissa fought their arms, feeling like she was being constricted and measured. She loved wearing sweaters because they hid how fat she felt. She now realized the bulk had also hidden the weight she had lost. She had worked so hard to lose those pounds. They couldn't criticize her for that. She squirmed in their hold, still crying. Then she collapsed against her parents.

When she gathered her breath, what must have been at least ten minutes later, Dad lowered her back into her chair.

"We're ready to listen, Mel, if you're ready to talk."

Why was she crying? Because of butter on a bagel? Because she couldn't go to school or practice? Because Todd certainly wouldn't pick her for captain now? Because of Beau? Where should she start? What should she say?

"It's everything! You wouldn't understand!" she blurted.

"You've got a lot going on." Mom nodded with compassion.

"I can't go to practice today, and now I know I won't make captain!"

"Because you'll miss one practice?" Dad asked, angling his brows.

"No. Yes. No." Melissa tilted her head from side to side. "Because Todd sent me home yesterday, and he won't think the kind of girl who's sent home from practice is the kind of girl who could lead his team next year." Melissa kicked off her saddles, letting them thud on the floor. She didn't feel worthy to wear them. "He won't even let me perform tonight."

"Let's talk about that," Mom offered. "Why did Todd send you home?"

There was nothing she could make up that would make sense. Todd said she couldn't come back until she'd seen a doctor. She would have to come clean.

"I fainted."

"And," Dad probed.

"That's it. I fainted, and Todd overreacted and thinks I need to see a doctor. He won't let me perform until I do." Melissa nibbled on her nails. "I guess we'd better call Dr. Ferrone, right?"

Mom glanced at the clock on the stove.

"I called her office when we got home yesterday. You have an appointment in an hour."

Melissa couldn't believe it. It wasn't like she was sick.

"And," Mom continued, "I called Todd last night to see why he was so bent on you seeing a doctor."

Melissa dropped her eyes to her shoes under the table.

"He thinks you're not eating, sweetie," Mom whispered.

Everything got blurry as large tears gushed from Melissa's eyes.

"I eat," she squeaked.

"I have to admit, I haven't been paying attention to what you eat, Mel," Dad chimed in. "I assume you're old enough to know when you're hungry and what's good for you. You always have breakfast before we wake up and lunch at school. Dinner just depends on our schedules, and between your practices, Mom's volunteering, and my crazy deadlines, we only eat together a couple of times a week." He put his hand on her hand. "I'm sorry."

"Whatever, it's not a big deal," Melissa sputtered between the tears that kept falling. How could Dad blame this on not eating dinner together?

"It's not anyone's fault," Mom said, placing her hand on Melissa's other hand. "But we're all in this together. We'll find a way to fix things."

Chapter Twenty-Two

Melissa wished Mom had stayed in the waiting room. She felt uncomfortable undressing in front of her. She knew it was her own mother, but it was still kind of weird. And today she knew Mom would be scrutinizing her. She turned toward the wall when she pulled off her sweater and quickly pulled the paper gown around her.

Mom gasped. "Mel, you're just a skeleton!"

Melissa turned back around and only now, with the gown partially covering her legs, slid off her jeans.

"Hardly," Melissa said.

The room was cold. Goosebumps crept down Melissa's arms and legs. The harsh smell of rubbing alcohol stung her nose.

Rap rap rap.

A middle-aged nurse with cropped salt-and-pepper hair, clear glasses with partial frames, and tangerine-colored lipstick stuck her head in the room.

"Good morning." Mom smiled.

"Morning," the nurse grumbled, looking over Melissa's chart. She sat on the cracked black leather stool and spun toward the desk. "Are you fourteen?" the nurse interrogated without looking up.

"Uh-huh." Melissa looked to Mom. Was this lady going to even look at her?

"And you're here today because . . ."

Melissa shrugged.

After a cold silence, the nurse looked up and slid her glasses back on her nose. When she got no answer from Melissa, she turned toward Melissa's mom.

"Melissa has had some fainting spells at dance practice. We just wanted to make sure everything was okay."

The nurse scribbled noisily in the file.

Melissa shivered. It was freezing in this room!

"Come with me." The nurse rose, opened the door, and stepped into the hallway.

Mom nodded to Melissa, then stood and followed.

"Put your feet on the footprints." The nurse indicated two bright blue footprints painted on the base of the scale. Melissa had always thought it was cool when she was younger to align her feet exactly on the prints. It didn't feel fun today. Nothing about scales seemed fun anymore. She knew she would weigh more than she wanted and less than her mom wanted. What if Mom tried to get her to gain weight after she had agonized for so long over losing it?

The nurse announced the weight to anyone within hearing distance and noted the numbers in the chart.

"Turn around," she ordered like an army lieutenant.

Melissa turned so her back rested against the cold

metal bar.

"Five feet, nine inches," the nurse announced, slapping the folder shut. "The doctor will be with you shortly." She tightened her lips and waddled away.

Melissa followed Mom back into the examining room and rolled her eyes. "You would think if you chose to be a pediatric nurse, you might like kids."

"Be nice." Mom laughed.

Melissa waited for Mom to comment on her weight, but she didn't.

"Remember when you were little and you always hoped you would get this room?"

Melissa, flooded by a memory, relaxed for a moment. Each of the rooms was a different color. Today they were in the yellow room. She had been so proud as a toddler when the nurse had asked her to find the yellow room and she could run right to it. The walls were covered in canary-colored cartoon ducks with orange beaks. She hadn't even noticed they were in her favorite room. She hadn't noticed much going on around her lately.

Dr. Ferrone stuck her head in the door. When Melissa was little, Dr. Ferrone would open a plastic box she kept hidden in the desk drawer and wink one of her sparkling gray eyes as a signal that Melissa could select a sticker to wear home. When Melissa was eleven and fell out of a tree, Dr. Ferrone let Melissa choose the color of cast for her broken elbow. Melissa picked yellow, and Dr. Ferrone had confided that yellow was her favorite color too.

"Good morning, ladies."

Melissa pulled her fingernails from her mouth to shake the doctor's outstretched hand.

"So you've been feeling kind of dizzy?" Dr. Ferrone leaned onto her swivel stool and smiled. Fine lines now framed those sparkling gray eyes.

Melissa nodded. "Some."

"Let's find out what's going on."

After listening to Melissa's heart, looking in her ears, making her follow a flashlight with her eyes, taking her blood pressure, having her say, "Ahhh," and asking a list of questions about everything from nosebleeds to stomachaches, Dr. Ferrone leaned back. This whole routine seemed pretty generic . . . until Dr. Ferrone asked, "Melissa, how many times a day do you check your weight?"

"Usually just twice . . . why?"

Dr. Ferrone paused, looking at mother and daughter. "Neither of you will want to hear this, but both of you need to."

Melissa's fingernails flew back to her teeth. What was she going to say?

"In America, as many as ten million females and one million males are fighting a battle with a life-threatening eating disorder. I believe Melissa is one of them."

Melissa saw her mom's eyes grow wide. Melissa sat still, gnawing on a nail.

"I wouldn't classify you as anorexic," the doctor continued, nodding to Melissa, "but we have a problem we need to address before things spin out of control."

Melissa's knee bounced up and down. Tears welled up in her eyes. She kept her gaze forward. She couldn't look at Mom.

"Melissa, you need to know that your weight and your control of your weight is a symptom, not the problem. Mrs. Rollins, it's very important you understand this too."

One tear spilled out of Melissa's right eye. Her left index finger remained clenched between her teeth. She felt her face contort. An eating disorder? Right! She was just trying to be thin. Thin like Gracie and Lindsey. They didn't have "disorders." Thin like the rest of the dance team, thin like all of the pretty girls, so Beau would like her.

"Have you had a lot of stress or pressure lately?" Dr. Ferrone furrowed her brow at Melissa.

Melissa looked at the wall and then down. "Well, a little, nothing major, just, you know, school and stuff."

"She and her boyfriend broke up," Mom blurted out. "Sorry, Mel, but it's true. Plus, you have officer tryouts for dance, and your schoolwork seems a lot more demanding than last year."

Melissa bounced both knees now. She brushed away another stray tear.

"Thanks, Mom." She tried to laugh sarcastically.

"A lot of changes come with high school, Melissa. Those changes can cause stress, but being under pressure doesn't justify what you're doing to yourself. You can't deprive your body of the nutrients and calories it needs to function." Dr. Ferrone swiveled on her black stool. "Your mom mentioned schoolwork being overwhelming. Your brain needs certain foods to think and stay focused. She also said something about dance. You know you need calories to give you energy for that kind of exercise."

Melissa nodded and flipped her hair back. "But I eat," she retorted. "I eat three meals every day."

"I'm sure you do," Dr. Ferrone almost whispered. "The problem is, you don't seem to be eating enough. Let's start with breakfast. What do you typically eat?"

Melissa regained a little composure. "A blueberry bagel, sometimes, a banana and orange juice." Her voice quivered, but she ticked them off on her fingers confidently.

"Good, Melissa. That does sound healthy. But do you ever, say, water down your orange juice? Or have you ever secretly discarded food to make people think you're eating when you're not? Or would you ever do something like induce vomiting?"

Melissa looked to the floor. Out of the corner of her eye, she saw her mom's hand silently clasp an open mouth.

Dr. Ferrone shook her head. "Two-thirds of all eating disorders are actually obsessive/compulsive disorders. It seems this is the root of Melissa's problem. When everything else seems to be spinning out of control, Melissa controls her food."

The doctor rolled her chair close to Melissa and put one hand on hers. She looked up at her and asked, "What do you think? Did I get any of it right?"

Melissa just kept her eyes on the floor—wishing she was under it right now—trying to avoid her pediatrician's compassionate gaze.

Dr. Ferrone leaned back and clapped her hands together. "Okay, ladies, here's what we're going to do. We need to take things slowly. First, I'll write a note excusing Melissa from school for the next week. That will give us a chance to start combating this thing. Second, you two need to come back here one week from today—that's next Friday—and Melissa will need to gain three pounds between now and then."

Three pounds! She knew it. Melissa had done all of that work for nothing. She looked to her mom to see if she was buying all of this. Mom was watching the doctor intently, nodding her head. Melissa then knew she was outnumbered; she would never win against Mom, Dad, *and* Dr. Ferrone. But deep down, she was almost relieved for someone else to be in on her secret, someone else to be in control.

"You both have separate assignments. Mrs. Rollins, either you or your husband need to eat every meal with Melissa. I know you're busy, and you all are probably used to eating on the fly, but it is very important to establish consistent eating rituals. Now, don't use these times to play police." Dr. Ferrone smiled. "Just spend mealtime as a social time to ensure everyone is having meals."

Melissa saw Mom nod and lick her lips. She saw the wheels spinning inside Mom's head as she mapped out their new routine.

"Your job, young lady," Dr. Ferrone said to Melissa, patting her hand, "is to eat and to take a break from exercise."

Melissa nodded. "I already eat. No big deal."

"Well, you're going to have to eat more than you're eating now in order to gain three pounds by the next time you see me," Dr. Ferrone answered. "And if you don't, I'll have no choice but to send you to a clinic for evaluation, potentially even to be checked in for treatment."

Melissa felt a wave of nausea. The back of her throat burned. A clinic? Treatment?

"But if you *can* gain the weight, I'll refer you to a counselor so you can start sorting things out."

As they walked to the car, Melissa put her left hand up to her head with her index finger and thumb shaped like the letter L. "Loser," she whispered, not being able to say anything else without losing control.

"You're not a loser," Mom assured her. She shoved the literature on eating disorders into her purse and wrapped her arm around her daughter. Melissa felt trapped by the weight of Mom's arm. She didn't want to be babied. She didn't have a problem. She just had a lot going on.

Chapter Twenty-Three

Mom pulled the bean burrito, diet soda, and tortilla chips from the paper bag and set them in front of Melissa. Melissa stared at all of the fatty food in front of her. She winced just thinking about eating sour cream and cheese. Mom sat down and waited. Melissa felt Mom's eyes on her. She willed Mom to stop staring. It didn't work. How could she eat or even move under such scrutiny? She took a sip from her straw to look busy. The bubbles calmed her stomach. She looked at Mom, tilted her head, and smiled weakly.

They chitchatted about everything except Melissa's eating disorder as Mom polished off her soft taco smothered in hot sauce and Melissa ate a few forkfuls of black beans and nibbled at the edges of her tortilla.

She started to wrap up the mostly uneaten lunch back in its foil wrapper as Mom planned all the fun things they could do with Melissa's week off from school.

"Wait a minute, sweetie. You barely touched your food. I thought you loved El Munchitos!"

"I do, Mom. I'm just not that hungry, okay? It's been kind of a rough morning," Melissa snapped. Then she

shook her head and said, "Month, actually."

"Okay," Mom agreed, but her eyes showed concern. "Try to eat more at dinner?"

"Deal."

The next few meals were like that. Mom bought or cooked something fattening, and Melissa was grossed out by the overwhelming gooeyness or greasiness of the food.

On Saturday night Melissa felt like she was going to throw up when Dad lifted the lid of the white cardboard box to reveal a super-stuffed pizza with all the toppings. She turned away and tensed her jaw as he pulled a piece onto a plate.

"Mel, you've got to eat something," Dad pleaded when he saw her cringe.

"Yeah, something, Dad, but not *that*. I'm trying, really, but that's gross! That pizza's so loaded with fat and cholesterol and calories and carbs. I mean, who really eats sausage and pepperoni and double cheese and hamburger all at once? It could give you a heart attack!"

Dad nodded. "I get it. Would a slice of plain cheese work?"

Melissa inhaled and closed her eyes. *God, please help! Where are You?*

A wave of calm filled her.

"I'll try."

Dad picked up the phone and ordered a small cheese pizza. It tasted surprisingly yummy. In fact, Melissa ate a whole piece. She almost grabbed a second slice but stopped herself. She and her parents were laughing by the end of dinner. It felt nice to be a person again, for food to taste good, to laugh, and not to be worried about school, friends, or Beau for just a night.

After dinner the phone rang.

"Hello?"

"Hey, Yellow." Gracie's voice seemed to smile.

"Hey."

"So is everything all right? When you weren't at school yesterday I called, but your mom said you were sick, and you didn't call back. Lindsey said you passed out at practice. Are you okay?"

"Yeah." Melissa curled her legs around herself in the wooden kitchen chair. "I'm such a loser for fainting! What did Lindsey say?"

"I don't know, just that you passed out and Todd kind of freaked out and sent you home and made her tell your mom to take you to the doctor. We've all been totally worried."

"I didn't mean to scare you. With Beau and school and everything, I just hadn't felt like eating much, and I got kind of dizzy. No big deal."

"You've always been kind of dizzy," Gracie teased.

"Thanks a lot." Melissa laughed.

"So why the doc?"

"Just to make sure it wasn't anything big." Melissa paused. "And it's not. She just wants me to stay home for a week to get my strength up. Anyway, I'll need you to one, fill me in on all the gossip, and two, help me get caught up in French—in that order, of course."

Chapter Twenty-Four

Melissa spent the week with Mom, who cancelled all of her social and volunteer obligations. She felt like she was five years old. They went to the mall and to the grocery store. Melissa got to pick out foods that sounded good to her like salads and fruit—things she could eat without feeling overwhelmed.

After school every day Gracie came over and brought Melissa's assignments and books. They sat and chatted in the family room for at least an hour sipping diet sodas.

"So, Yellow, how *are* you?" Gracie asked every day.

"Fine, everything's great—really great. What could be better than getting the week off from school and not even being sick? Right?" Melissa grinned and nodded. She hated lying to Gracie. She knew her best friend could see right through her. Gracie and the rest of the crew must suspect something. It was weird that she had to stay home for a week when she looked and acted normal, but she couldn't tell them, not even Gracie.

By Wednesday Melissa was bored of lounging around the house. She had really focused on her homework and gotten caught up in all of her classes. She stretched and practiced her dance moves every day, as if she were at real practice, since Dr. Ferrone and Todd had both made it clear they wouldn't let her go back yet. She painted her toes electric blue and her fingernails shocking pink, and she even organized all of her photos and music on her computer.

When Melissa woke up Thursday morning, she shuffled in slow motion, went to the bathroom, and took off her pajamas. Naked, she stood on the scale.

"Two pounds," she said aloud. Two pounds wasn't awful, but it was so much work to lose them and way too easy to gain them back. She stepped off the scale. Sometimes if she waited for a minute, she could weigh back in at a lighter weight.

Then Melissa remembered. She screamed, covering her mouth with her hand. She stepped to the sink and in a frenzy brushed her teeth. "Maybe the toothpaste will add something," she mumbled to herself. She slathered herself with lotion and exhaled.

She stepped back on and held her breath. Her eyes grew as wide as waffles. Now the scale teetered between a one- and two-pound gain. Melissa's heart thumped like the bass on Todd's speakers. She tossed on jeans and a yellow sweatshirt and scampered down the stairs.

"Mom!" she cried.

Mom wasn't in the kitchen.

"*MOM!*"

She wasn't in the family room, the dining room, or the living room. Melissa scanned every room. Her palms grew sweaty. Her neck prickled.

"What is it, sweetie?" Mom ran through the laundry room door with a basket of clean clothes. Her face was pale and panicked. "What's wrong?"

Melissa stared wide-eyed at Mom, her mouth hung open like *The Scream* by Edvard Munch, and she began to bawl. She felt like the person depicted in that painting—all alone, stranded, and misshapen.

Mom put down the laundry, and Melissa collapsed into her. She was relieved Mom didn't ask any questions. She didn't have any answers or any words. After several minutes Melissa pulled her head up enough to eke out, "Mom?"

"What is it, Mel?" Mom whispered.

"Dr. Ferrone. You know how she said I had to gain three pounds?" She choked back a sob. "By tomorrow?"

"Yeah."

"What do you think will happen if I don't?"

Mom breathed deeply, stepped back, and looked her daughter in the eye. "How much have you gained, Melissa?"

"Two pounds. I mean, I stepped on the scale, and it said I'd gained two, but I stepped on again after I brushed my teeth and lotioned up and it said I gained one. Which is really weird because toothpaste and lotion add weight," she rambled.

Mom laughed sympathetically and hugged Melissa tighter. "You thought you could gain weight by brushing your teeth or putting on lotion? Honey!"

Melissa wiped the saltwater smears from her face with the back of her hand and snorted. She shook her head. "What am I going to do? Mom, she can't send me away. I can't go to a *clinic*."

"We're going to get you up to three pounds by tomorrow. Now, I know you get worked up about eating, and I don't want to stress you out, but we're going to sit down right now and eat breakfast." Mom squeezed Melissa. Even though her mom was small-framed, Melissa felt her mother's strength.

Melissa nodded.

"You can have your normal bagel and watered-down orange juice. But you're going to eat a banana, too."

Melissa nodded again. That sounded reasonable. And to avoid the clinic, she would do almost anything.

"And then . . ." Mom put her arm around Melissa's shoulder and guided her into the kitchen. "After you've looked over some of your homework, we're going to make chocolate chip cookies." Mom's eyes twinkled.

Melissa grinned and twirled her hair up into a knot, loose strands floating to the floor. By now, she ignored the wads of dark silk, which seemed to fall out whenever she moved. She could never resist chocolate chips, cookie dough, or fresh-from-the-oven cookies. But they were so fattening, so full of sugar, so full of carbs. There wasn't anything about them that fit into her diet or into who she had become. She took a bite of banana and vowed to eat the whole thing. That would be a better way to make weight.

Chapter Twenty-Five

While studying, Melissa noticed her Bible on her nightstand. Even though she'd been home all week, she hadn't even touched the soft leather cover. She had been so upset with her parents, her doctor, and herself. She had been so scared of what would happen if she didn't eat and then what would happen if she did. Would she get fat again? Would Beau or any boy ever think she was cute? Would she even make the dance team next year as a heavy sophomore? She wasn't ready to face God and His judgment on her. But there He was, waiting by her bedside.

Melissa knew down somewhere deep it always felt good to read the Bible, to pray, to talk to God. She plopped down on her comforter and lifted the heavy book. She opened the pages to where her bookmark kept the place of her last reading, Luke 16.

"Oh, yeah, the eating scraps passage. I knew God would try to punish me for all of this."

Melissa was so angry she felt like daring God. She decided to read the verses over again and tell Him a thing or two about eating and all of the pressures surrounding her, but as she read her shoulders relaxed and her fingers fell from between her teeth. She leaned back against her pillow and read again.

A tear trickled slowly down her left cheek. She hadn't read the whole thing before, and she certainly hadn't heard God's words until now. The point of the story was not about food at all. The point was that she needed Jesus, *now*. She couldn't wait for another day or for someone else to warn her about the bad stuff in life. The rich man who had been condemned wanted to warn his family and friends to change their ways, but Jesus said He'd given them the tools to know right from wrong for themselves.

The poor man had gone to heaven, but not because he had only eaten scraps. He went to heaven because he believed. The Bible didn't say she needed to eat scraps. Instead it said she needed to get rid of the things in her life that separated her from Jesus, which for Melissa wasn't eating at all; it was *not* eating!

Her obsession with food had hindered her from sharing things with her parents, Gracie, Lindsey, and the rest of the crew. It had prevented her from going to practice and school this whole week, and it had even distanced her from God!

Right there on her bed, Melissa bowed her head. She finally had the courage to pray—to pray for the right things.

Dear God, I have been so stupid! All I wanted was to make captain and for Beau to like me and for my friends to like me and to keep up at school. Melissa laughed at herself. *Okay, I wanted all kinds of stuff. But I wasn't trying to be greedy. I just thought all that stuff would make me happy. Then everything got crazy! The food, the not talking to anyone, Beau. Anyway, God, I'm sorry. I'm really, really sorry.* She had to take a deep breath. The tears slid down her face.

I hope You'll forgive me. I know You will because You forgive everything, but I don't know why. Anyway, please make me a better person. Please help me eat enough so I don't need to go to a clinic, so I can be normal again. I just want to be normal again. She wiped her tears with her sleeve and hugged her knees to her chest.

I don't have to be captain, and I don't have to get Beau back, but I don't want to be so stressed and crazy all of the time. I just want to do my best and to take care of myself however You want me to. 'Cause after all, You're the One who made me. Amen.

Melissa didn't have any more words or any more tears. She felt an unusual calmness like floating on a raft in the ocean—no outside distractions, the world's sounds muted by the lulling waves, just a gentle rocking. She swayed back and forth on her bed, clutching her body in a safe ball, relishing the relief from all the turmoil that had filled her for months. She lifted her head and took a deep breath.

"Chocolate chippers!" The smell of fresh-baked cookies filled her nose. Her tummy growled like a lion spying a gazelle. She patted her stomach and laughed.

Melissa walked into her bathroom, splashed cold water on her face, and bounded down the stairs two at a time.

"Do I smell cookies?" she called.

/ / /

The cookies seemed to send Melissa on an upward spiral. She scarfed down two and washed them down with a huge glass of milk. They tasted delicious. She actually enjoyed the act of eating them. It was like a huge burden had been lifted, the burden to be responsible for everything, even every calorie. She knew God was taking some of that burden from her. And it felt good. At lunch she ate two pieces of leftover pizza and at dinner had a huge wedge of bubbling lasagna with her salad, instead of just the salad. She felt ravenous and everything tasted so amazing, so spicy and sweet and tangy, so much more than it ever had before.

The next morning, all of her eating paid off when she stood on the scales at Dr. Ferrone's.

"Three pounds exactly," Dr. Ferrone remarked, scribbling on her chart.

Melissa rolled her eyes and smiled in relief.

"Well done, but you're not off the hook. You may resume normal activities, but you need to gain two more pounds by next week and set up a meeting with the counselor I mentioned." Dr. Ferrone handed a white business card to Melissa's mom.

Melissa swallowed hard. She had made it, but she

had binged to gain those pounds. She had to be good today. Her toes tapped frantically on the linoleum floor. *Dear God, how can I do this?* She pictured herself on a raft again, the sun beating down on her bare shoulders. She truly tried to listen to Him.

With Me, that's how. She seemed to hear. *I'll help you do this.*

Dr. Ferrone turned to Melissa's mom. "Same rules apply. You or your husband need to keep track of your daughter's intake." She looked up from her paperwork and peered over her silver spectacles. "Melissa's done a great job, and so have you, but she's a long way from recovered. This is a battle that may be with her the rest of her life."

Melissa furrowed her brow and tilted her head. She could gain two more pounds if she had to, but when would this end? How could this not be over?

"Melissa, gaining the weight is one step in the right direction." Dr. Ferrone put her hand on Melissa's still bony shoulder. "But you exhibit obsessive/compulsive behavior. You will probably always have that personality trait, and you will be challenged to manage it properly. If you're not careful, eating is something you may continue to obsess and be compulsive about forever." The doctor motioned for her to get off the scale and to sit in one of the plastic chairs.

"We'll try to teach you how to find the right balance in your diet. The rest of the road is a long one, but you're on the right track. Remember, two more pounds by next week. After that we'll start some education for your family on getting the right amounts of the right foods to maintain a healthy weight."

"Okay." Melissa turned her thumb to get the edge of her nail between her teeth, but her hand shook too hard.

Dr. Ferrone patted Melissa on the back and left the room.

This was more than Melissa had expected. She'd done so much. She'd eaten so much, and now the overwhelming goal of "forever" loomed.

"Mom?" she tried to ask, but tears instead of words flowed.

Her mom had tears in her eyes too. "We'll take it one step at a time, Melissa. You, Dad and I, and God—we're all in this together."

Chapter Twenty-Six

Beeeep beeeep beeeep beeeep.

Melissa turned off the alarm. She wiggled her toes under the covers. This was it—Saturday morning practice. The day she'd been waiting for. The day she joined the rest of the world. Mom and Dad were great, but she missed her friends. She missed school. She missed Beau; well, she wouldn't go there. But most of all, she missed dancing.

She hopped out of bed. If she was going to show Todd she was okay, she needed to eat breakfast. She'd probably blown her chance at captain, but she still wanted Todd to think she was an asset to his team.

Downstairs she toasted a whole bagel, grabbed a whole banana, and put a little less water and a little more juice in her glass. She felt like a kernel of popcorn in a pot of hot oil. She couldn't stand still. Everyone going to be watching her to see if she would faint again or if there was something truly wrong with her. Maybe she shouldn't go.

"Good morning, pumpkin," Dad murmured on the way to the coffeepot. "I thought I'd join you before you go off to resume the life of a normal teenager."

"Thanks, Dad," she said. And meant it. She'd hated the way her parents had lurked at every meal, but today it was comforting to have someone with her. Somehow Dad seemed more bearable than Mom. He knew fewer details of what had been going on. He asked fewer questions.

"Since I'm up, I thought I might as well give you a ride to practice. It's freezing—eighteen degrees." He poured steaming coffee in his mug. The rich aroma filled the air with the promise of a new start. "Plus, I'd really like to see the *New York Times* this morning. I'm going to go out and get one."

"Great. Thanks." Melissa sat down and started working on her breakfast. She still had to concentrate on taking each bite, chewing each bite, and swallowing each bite, but she managed to finish it all.

Dad pulled into the church from the front. Melissa usually went in the back way, but Dad drove a different route than Melissa walked so he could pick up his newspaper. As their headlights beamed on the stained-glass cross, it struck her that all this time she had been practicing at church. God had been with her every time Jill made fun of her and every time she misstepped. God had even been there when she fainted, but she hadn't seen Him. She hadn't really been looking for Him.

"I know you'd rather practice at the school gym, but it is kind of cool you get to have rehearsals the same place we pray," Dad commented while turning the wheel.

It was like he'd read her mind.

"Yeah." Melissa nodded. "It's kind of nice."

"What time do you get done?" Dad asked.

"Ten."

"I'll come back and pick you up. I'll be done reading this by then." He held up his paper and winked.

"You don't have to." Melissa slid out the door.

"I don't have to, but I want to," Dad said. "You forget, we dads like to take care of our little girls too, even when they're not so little."

"Okay." Melissa rolled her eyes and laughed. "See ya."

She walked toward the heavy doors, then her heart hiccupped. She bent down to pretend to tie her shoe, stalling. She stood again with no more excuses to stay outside in the cold. Pushing the door open, she breathed in the smell of church, candle wax, new carpeting, old books. Facing Todd and the team wasn't going to be easy, but Melissa felt better knowing God would be there too.

Melissa walked into the half-lit gym. Her footsteps echoed eerily in the big empty room. She was the first one there.

Dear God, I know You're here. Please help me. I'm nervous. What will everyone say? What has everyone been saying? I hope Todd doesn't send me home, but he might. I mean, he probably will tell me to forget the whole captain thing.

Slam!

The side door banged shut as Todd made his entrance lugging music, coffee, and his workout bag.

"Girlfriend!" he yelled, running to Melissa and somehow hugging her with his hands full. "How have you been? I want to hear everything." He managed to hold Melissa's hand while he waltzed over to the sound system and started setting up shop.

Melissa relaxed her jaw. "I'm great! Really great! I'm so glad to be back." Melissa remembered the note from Dr. Ferrone in her bag, allowing her to return to practice. "Oh yeah, wait a second." She released Todd's hand and ran to her bag. By now some of the other girls were arriving.

"Here's the note"—she lowered her voice—"from my doctor. You know, saying I'm okay."

"Thanks!" Todd snatched the note, looked over it, and clapped his hands.

"Ladies, let's get to it!" He punched the play button on the sound system, and the opening chords echoed through the gym.

Melissa tried to ignore the pairs of eyes glued on her. She somehow had to make up for a week of downtime, and she wasn't going to do that by letting anyone get to her. *Focus*, she reminded herself.

Melissa kicked, turned, stomped, and jumped. She smiled and swirled and swiveled. She had more energy than she'd had in weeks, and her performance showed it. She messed up a couple of times, forgetting a step here and there and not knowing a part of the routine that had changed while she was out, but she did okay.

"That's a wrap!" shouted Todd. "See y'all on Monday."

Melissa's whole body felt tickly, like she'd guzzled a bottle of Sprite. She collapsed on the bench next to Stacey.

"So, you okay?" Stacey asked between gulps from her water bottle.

"Yeah, great!" Melissa beamed. "At least until Todd beat us up."

They laughed. No one else asked about Melissa's fainting or absence. She had done it! It felt great to be herself again. Now she knew she could get through dance. The next thing she had to get through was facing everyone at school—including Beau.

Chapter Twenty-Seven

*M*elissa woke up Monday morning, went to the bathroom, took off her pj's, and got on the scale before eating or brushing her teeth. Her habits weren't going to break that quickly. Her weight lingered where it had the last two days. "I guess a whole banana isn't too treacherous after all," she said to herself with a smile.

Melissa looked in the mirror. Her belly seemed to bulge. Her eyes sunk into their sockets. Her once thick mane of hair was stringy and lifeless. She turned away. Everything was wrong with her! She still felt fat and ugly. Hot tears filled the rims of her eyes.

She took a series of deep breaths and then turned to the one Person who could help. *God, I need You. I cannot do this. Not without You. I need You to help me. I want to take care of myself. I want to be over this, but it seems like I never will be.* Melissa walked out of the bathroom and wiped the tears trickling down her cheeks. She felt calmer and stronger, less shaky. *I felt good at practice Saturday. I really did. And church was awesome yesterday. I can do this with You.*

Melissa was really starting to believe her conversation with God as she pulled on her jeans, stiff from the dryer. She didn't feel brave, but she wasn't petrified either. She pulled on her favorite yellow sweater. It somehow made her feel thin and confident and even seemed to make her hair look shinier and sleeker.

She went downstairs to find Mom and Dad sitting at the breakfast table. Her bagel, banana, and juice were made and waiting for her.

She looked from Mom to Dad. She had grown accustomed to having a watchdog at meals, but both of them was a bit much.

Dad shrugged. "We decided we kind of like getting up early."

"And we definitely like starting our day together," Mom said, handing everyone a napkin. "Dad and I even thought we could start praying as a family in the mornings to get centered before we all go our separate ways."

Melissa nodded as she slid into her seat.

Mom sat down next to her and said, "Well, let's see. Should we hold hands?"

Melissa, Dad, and Mom formed a circle. Dad's hand was rough and hairy but warm and large and comforting. Mom's smooth, cold, slender fingers squeezed Melissa's as she began to pray. "Dear God, please be with us today. Please be with Tom as he goes to work that he may maintain Christian values in the workplace. Please be with me as I go to tennis that I may refrain from gossip and stay true to You. And please be with Mel as she goes back to school. Let her know that You love her and that we love her too." Mom tried to act casual, but she choked up at the end of the prayer. Melissa's eyes misted too. Even Dad cleared his throat before saying, "Amen."

"Thanks," Melissa whispered and then bit into her bagel. Before she could finish her banana, Tanner's horn honked from the driveway. Her heart raced. She was supposed to eat all of her food. That was the program, but here he was, and he and Gracie would be waiting. Her face flushed.

"Sweetie, why don't you have one last swig of juice and take your banana with you in the car?" Mom cheerily offered.

Melissa's shoulders relaxed. The answer was that simple. "What would I do without you, Mom?"

She slid on her coat, slipped her backpack onto her shoulders, and took a long swallow of cold juice. She popped the last bite of sweet bagel into her mouth.

"Bye, Dad. Bye, Mom. Thanks for the prayer, too," she mumbled, chewing her food.

She scampered out the door and hopped in the backseat of Tanner's Mustang, holding her half-eaten banana. Gracie and Tanner looked back and smiled, but both were jamming so much they didn't speak. "Big House" by Audio Adrenaline was blaring on the radio. A smile spread across Melissa's face. Her head started to bob back and forth to the beat. Her shoulders swayed from side to side. She joined her friends, singing at the top of her lungs. By the time the threesome pulled into the school parking lot, Melissa felt different. She almost strutted out of the car. The music had elevated her mood. Music always did that to her. That was why she loved to dance.

In front of the big silver doors, she pulled Gracie to the side. "Okay, Gray, it's time I came clean."

Gracie tilted her head. "I've been hoping you would."

"I need your help," Melissa continued. "I mean, I'm sure you know there's something up with me being out of school a whole week and everything."

Gracie nodded.

"Well, I, well, it's just that I wasn't eating enough. I mean, it's no big deal or anything." Melissa smiled and waved at some girls on the dance team coming through the doors. "It's just with Beau and Chemistry and these silly officer tryouts, I just kind of, well, got stressed and stopped eating enough. So I got dizzy and weak, and I'm perfectly fine now, but . . ." Melissa rambled until she reached the hardest part.

"But what?" Gracie asked. She looked concerned.

"But I need your help," Melissa spit out. "I need you to be, like, my secret partner. Just to make sure I eat everything I bring." Melissa motioned to her backpack. "See, I need to pack a lunch to make sure I'm getting enough calories, so please don't let everyone make fun of me for packing my lunch." Melissa faked a smirk and drew her right ring finger to her teeth.

"Hey! I really wanted to start packing a lunch too!" Gracie's eyes widened. "I need to save up some money to get Drew a birthday present, and I figured if I packed a lunch, I could stash my lunch money, but I don't know, everyone else buys something in the cafeteria, so I just felt stupid."

"Well, now we can be stupid together." Melissa grinned.

Gracie leaned closer to Melissa. "I was worried about you, you know. And, yes, I promise to be your secret agent and your brown-bagger buddy."

Melissa hugged Gracie.

Gracie squeezed back and whispered, "But mostly I promise to be your best friend."

"I'd be lost without you," Melissa whispered.

Brrring! The bell signaled six minutes until class.

"Bye!" Melissa waved to Gracie as she ran toward her locker. *Thanks, God. Thanks for giving me Mom and Dad and Gracie to help me through. Together, we can all do this!*

Chapter Twenty-Eight

When Melissa slid into her desk in French class, she was relieved to see Beau wasn't there. When he wasn't in Algebra either, she knew he was absent. That relieved a lot of her first-day-back pressure.

On Tuesday she had a little more confidence. Melissa had gotten through the first day without any major glitches, Gracie made a great conspirator, and Todd said she could perform at tonight's basketball halftime with the rest of the dance team.

She got to Monsieur Renauld's class two minutes early and systematically laid out her textbook, notebook, and pencil. Melissa wrote out a schedule for the rest of the day, including when and what she would eat, how long she would have to get ready for the game, and how she would squeeze homework into the hour when she first got home from school. As she erased and rewrote times to make everything on her agenda fit, she was interrupted.

"I'm glad you're back." Beau placed his warm hand on top of Melissa's.

Her heart stopped for a full second. Then it raced.

She couldn't breathe. Melissa had to force herself to swallow.

"Thanks." She couldn't bring herself to look into those dark brown eyes.

"Are you okay? I mean, is everything all right?" Beau's drawl sounded sincerely concerned.

His hand was still on her hand. She felt his warmth burning through her skin, leaving an achy feeling in her heart. "I'm fine, really." She found the courage to look up.

"Bonjour, messieurs et mademoiselles," Monsieur Renauld began. *"Monsieur Pointreaux, asseyez, s'il vous plaît?"*

Beau swiveled and sat. The smell of his soap was intoxicating. Melissa felt herself flush. He was so amazing. Why did she have to like him? And why did he have to act so concerned and touch her like that?

The class was repeating a phrase in French. Melissa forced herself to tune in to her teacher and tune out the handsome athlete in front of her.

At the sound of the bell, Melissa bolted to the bathroom. Gracie was only a half step behind her. Once inside the safety of the concrete room, Melissa leaned against the cool, hard wall, threw her head back, and closed her eyes.

"I can't believe he did that!" Melissa shrieked. "Who does he think he is?"

"I think he still likes you, Mel."

"Then why did he break up with me?"

"I don't know. Boys are weird." Gracie shrugged. "We'd better get to class. Update me at lunch, okay?"

Melissa nodded, took a deep breath, and ducked into the hallway. She managed to delay her entrance into Algebra long enough to avoid any more Beau interactions. She spent most of the day keeping a lookout for his dark curly hair. Whenever she sensed him, she turned up the level of whatever conversation she was having or just turned the corner and detoured around him.

This is crazy! she thought. *He was probably just being nice and doesn't even want to say anything else to me.*

At home, Melissa sped through her assignments and forced down an early dinner consisting of a grilled chicken breast with a dab of tangy barbeque sauce and a small helping of corn—no butter, of course. Mom lurked around the kitchen, serving as chaperone for the meal.

After she ate, Melissa put on her uniform. She pulled her hair back in a sparkly bow that matched the sequins on her costume. She polished her white boots until they shone. Melissa even applied a little sparkly eye shadow under her brow, some extra-shiny lip gloss, and a squirt of Love's Baby Soft perfume. The fresh, sweet smell that reminded her of baby powder and flowers made her feel like she was walking in a dream, lightheaded and worry free.

She loved the adrenaline rush before a performance. She hurried downstairs to get her letter jacket. Mom and Dad were waiting for her.

"What are you performing tonight?" asked Dad,

helping her with her coat.

"Oh, Dad, it's way cool. It's a jazz routine with a killer beat. You know that 80s tune I've been playing, 'Bizarre Love Triangle'?"

Dad nodded.

"I can't wait to see it," Mom said, grinning her June Cleaver smile. "Let's go."

During the first half of the game, Melissa sat with the dance team and the band. She gave Lindsey a yellow rose and a card saying she'd missed dancing with her. She felt guilty for not including Lindsey in her secret. She just wasn't ready to expose herself like that.

"Thanks, Yellow! You are just too sweet!" Lindsey squealed, hugging her.

"I've missed you, Linds. I just feel bad, that's all."

"Please! I'm just glad you're back. Now I have someone to gossip with during this boring game. By the way, I love the glitter!" Lindsey nodded her approval of Melissa's daring foray into the makeup world.

The crowd roared. Most of the Spring Hill side stood up. Beau had stolen the ball from the Lakota Lakers and was headed down to the home basket. He paused and aimed. The entire gymnasium was silent.

Swoosh!

He scored a three-pointer. The fans burst into applause, and the band trumpeted the fight song.

"How can I get my mind off Beau if he keeps doing things like that?" Melissa asked.

Lindsey leaned over and put her hand on Melissa's

thigh. She whispered, "This'll get your mind off that boy. Did you hear Todd yell at Jill for her poor attitude at practice?" She gave Melissa a nudge to the ribs. "Plus, everyone on the team was asking about you."

"Ladies!" Todd stamped his foot in the narrow walkway at the bottom of the bleachers.

Melissa and Lindsey scurried down the steps with the rest of the team to line up for their halftime show. When they got behind the bleachers, they filed into line and stood at attention, their chins in the air and their arms flat against their sides. They could hear the smack of gym shoes on the floor and the echo of the basketball bouncing, but they weren't allowed to move a muscle.

At the sound of the buzzer signaling the half, Alyssa blew her whistle in four short bursts, giving the girls the timing. They marched single file onto the gym floor and found their opening positions.

Tweet tweet tweet tweet. The whistle signaled the team to strike their pose and freeze.

Butterflies danced in Melissa's stomach. She'd only been to one practice since she'd been out. Lindsey had helped her with the routine, but was she ready for this?

Dear God, I need You now. I mean, I need You again.

The synthesizers boomed from the sound system, and Melissa slipped into her dream world of music and dance. She grinned and twisted and kicked and leaned. She jumped and swiveled until the music stopped and she hit her final pose. She had nailed it!

She could barely hear the whistle over the applause

from the stands.

Tweet tweet tweet tweet.

Melissa dropped her pose and marched out with the rest of her team. Once off the court she hugged Lindsey. Gracie ran up from behind them.

"Awesome, girls! Really awesome!"

Melissa beamed, then felt someone tap her shoulder. She turned to see Beau. He smelled like sweat, but it was a warm, rich sweat from a star athlete. Melissa felt woozy. The gym and Lindsey and Gracie all disappeared. It was just her and him.

"I just have a second. I'm not supposed to be away from the team." Beau sounded out of breath. "But I finally got to see you dance, and *WOW*!" He raised his eyebrows. "You were great!" Beau glanced behind his shoulder. The rest of the players were filing back into the gym for the second half. "Melissa, I'm crazy about you. My folks said as soon as basketball is over, I can maybe start to go out with you again. That is, if you still want to?" The coach was looking at the team. "Gotta run, but we still have tickets to the concert next week, right?" he shouted as he ran back to the bench.

Melissa stood, stunned, as her two friends jumped up and down, shrieking.

"That is so huge!" Gracie said, clutching Melissa's arm, bringing her back to reality. "I told you he still liked you."

"Way to go, Yellow," Lindsey joined in. "I think it's the glitter." She winked.

Melissa felt like she was soaring. She wasn't worrying about the next class or the next practice or the next meal. She was just happy, genuinely happy.

That night she flopped into bed, gathered her soft covers around her, and grabbed her Bible before turning out the light. She read Luke 12:22: "Do not worry about . . . what you will eat."

Why couldn't I have read that a long time ago? She laughed to herself.

Dear God, thank You. Thank You for showing me You are always there and for reminding me I can't do anything without You. A few months ago that made me feel weak and scared. I wanted to do it all myself. Now I know with You, it's way better. I have a long way to go. But I know I can get there with You. Amen.

Skinny Discussion Guide

Chapters 1–3

1. Whose comments influence the way Melissa views herself?

2. How do your comments to others affect their self-image?

3. Whose comments influence you?

4. After reading the following scripture passages:

   Proverbs 29:25
   Matthew 11:16-19
   1 Corinthians 4:3

   What do you think the Bible says about being yourself?

5. Whose comments do you think you should let influence you?

Chapters 4–6

1. What kind of pressures does Melissa feel from her parents? Her friends? School? The dance team? Beau?

2. Are these pressures real or self-imposed?

3. What areas of your life put demands on you?

4. Are these demands real or self-imposed?

5. After reading James 1:2-3, how do you think God expects you to handle the pressures of life?

Chapters 7–10

1. How much time does Melissa spend talking to God?

2. How much time does she spend listening to Him?

3. What does Philippians 4:1 say about praying?

4. How does Melissa try to take control of her life?

5. Read Galatians 3:5 and Romans 3:28 and discuss how important you feel it is to be in control?

Chapters 11–15

1. When do you see Melissa start to head downhill?

2. What are some of the things she does to lose weight?

3. Which ones seem extreme to you?

4. Do you know anyone who practices any of these methods to lose weight?

5. Have you ever tried any of these things to lose weight?

6. 1 Peter 3:3-4, says, "Don't be concerned about the outward beauty of fancy hairstyles, expensive jewelry, or beautiful clothes. . . . Clothe yourselves instead with the beauty that comes from within."

7. After reading this passage how do you think God feels about dieting?

Chapters 16–18

1. Describe Melissa's relationship with her Mom? With her Dad?

2. How is your relationship with your parents similar or dissimilar to Melissa's?

3. Exodus 20:12 states, "honor your father and mother". This one of the Ten Commandments is reiterated by Jesus in Matthew 19:19; Mark 10:19 and Luke 18:20. Knowing how important it is to God for us to honor our parents, can you think of any ways you could honor your parents better or more than you do today?

Chapter 19

1. Describe Melissa's relationship with Todd, her coach.

2. Do you have a coach/teacher/instructor/leader you could go to if you had a problem?

3. Who is it?

4. Who was the disciples' teacher/coach?

5. Do you think Jesus could counsel you through tough times as well?

Chapters 20–22

1. How does Melissa feel when she has to go see Dr. Ferrone?

2. How would you feel?

3. Read Luke 12:25 and discuss what things make you

feel anxious and how you can hand them over to the Lord.

4. If your doctor made you gain five pounds (or lose five pounds) before you could participate in any activities again, what would your reaction be?

5. The thought of gaining five pounds terrified Melissa. Read Psalm 34:4 and consider this: Could you gain (or lose) five pounds or do something else you're terrified of if asked?

Chapters 23–25

1. How did Melissa let the world drown out God's voice?

2. Have you ever misunderstood God or valued someone else's opinion over His?

3. Read Romans 7:15 and 24-25. Even the apostle Paul struggled with doing the right thing. Who does Paul say can help?

4. Do you believe Jesus can help you too?

Chapter 26–28

1. When Melissa turns everything over to God how does it change things?

2. Is there anything you need to turn over to God?

3. What's stopping you?

"If you had faith even as small as a mustard seed, you could say to this mountain, 'Move from here to there,' and it would move. Nothing would be impossible."

(Matthew 17:20)

Continue reading
Lindsey's story in Hot...

Chapter One

I changed my look this morning. I straightened my curls into poker-straight, shiny locks. I like it. It's sleek. The only problem is, without my curls my headband is too loose and keeps slipping off my head. I had to fix it in the girls' room between classes. So now I bolt toward English with seconds to spare.

As I scurry toward the door, I run smack into Noah Hornung. He's about twice as tall as me. He's running his fingers through his dark hair that seems to naturally spike up in a messy kind of way. He probably can't even see me from up there.

"Man, I am so sorry, Lindsey," he says in a rich voice that reminds me of the dark brown suede vest I splurged on last week.

"No problem." I crane my neck to look at him. How did he know my name, and has he always been that hot? I mean he's always been here. Noah goes to youth group with us at my best friend Emma's church. But so do a ton of other kids. And he always sits with a bunch of guys I hardly know. He lives in my sprawling subdivision, but on the other end. He's a junior, so even when we were kids and played in the neighborhood, he hung out with kids a year older than me. Noah's dark green eyes, topped by thick, dark eyebrows, lock with mine. I feel my cheeks turning as pink as my headband.

Brrriinnngg!

The class bell, announcing I am officially late, echoes through the vacant hallways.

"We're late," he laughs.

"Yeah, see ya." I cock my head and smile as I duck into my doorway.

Mrs. Pearson shoots me a dirty look as I try to sneak into my row.

I slide into my seat. My books softly thud on the desk. I lift my head to see Noah in the doorway winking at me before disappearing down the hall. Lights dance in my head, like flashbulbs of the paparazzi. His eyes are so big and my fingers itch to touch that messy hair. I don't know much about him, but I feel all tingly and freezing and burning at the same time, like my hand feels when I've held my hair dryer for too long. *Slow down,* I tell myself. *This is the first time he's ever spoken to you.*

I should relax, anyway. Boys and I put together have always been a "Fashion Don't." I've been asked on plenty of dates, but the boys all seem to want one thing: something physical. Nobody wants to listen to me or talk to me or even watch a movie with me. Sometimes I curse the fact that I'm pretty. I know it doesn't seem to make sense. I can't say that out loud to any of my friends. Who would understand?

I was so gawky when I was younger. I remember wishing I could look like my sister, Kristine, so that boys would notice me. Then, in eighth grade, I had eye surgery and said good-bye to my glasses. The orthodontist removed my braces. Kristine gave me a full makeover before I entered high school so I wouldn't embarrass her by being her "nerdy little sister." Now it seems like overnight, I'm not the geeky girl anymore. I've somehow evolved into the pretty girl I dreamed of being. It's so ironic. Now that I got my wish and people do think I'm pretty, I'm wishing for something else, that boys would be interested in *me*—what kind of music I listen to and what my thoughts on God are and how I feel about my family—instead of what I look like.

Tommy Bayer invited me to his house to watch a movie with his family. That seemed innocent enough. But it turned out his family wasn't even home. So about ten minutes into one of the *Shrek* movies, he leaned over and tried to stick his tongue down my throat. When I turned my face away from his, he turned from "Tommy Bayer" into "Tommy Bear" and tried to grab every part of my body he could with his grubby paws.

To prevent that from happening again, when Warren Adler asked me out, I suggested he come to *my* house. Wrong! He came over and kept trying to slide his hand in between my legs under the kitchen table. I squeezed my knees together so tight, my thighs ached by the time his mom came to take him home.

A beautiful boy named Brock invited me to our Christmas dance, the Sugarplum Stomp, last year. Mom bought me this amazing dress with a fitted waist. We had a seamstress take it in to fit perfectly, and it had a skirt that flared out just enough to *swoosh* while I was dancing. I told my friends I ended it with him because he popped his gum. The truth is, Brock tried to slip his hands into that gorgeous gown anywhere he thought they could fit.

Maybe I've just been interested in the wrong boys. The underclass guys seem unsure of themselves. They get all nervous and fidgety when they talk to me. Most of the upperclassmen seem so full of themselves. They act like they're doing me a favor if they speak to me.

Which brings me back to Noah. How did he even know my name? I still can't figure that out.

The fifty-minute class takes an eternity. Each second rigidly ticks on the black and white circular clock affixed above the door. I look out the door, half expecting to see Noah winking. I must be going crazy. Clearly, he's gone to class. I struggle to remain still. I have lots of practice from dance team. We are supposed to be like puppets, completely immobile until we're brought to life by music.

Mrs. Pearson lectures about the symbolism of Shakespeare and his description of Queen Mab. I doodle swirly designs on the borders of my spiral-bound notebook with my favorite aqua blue pen. My swirls are like the dreams described in the Shakespeare passage, hard to follow but seemingly purposeful.

At lunch my right foot nervously taps up and down by my plastic chair as I sit with my plate of French fries and a chocolate shake—about the only two things the cafeteria serves that I trust. I wait for my girlfriends to find their way to our table. The cafeteria smells like the old gum that's stuck under the tables and the mysterious gravy the cafeteria ladies ladle over suspiciously bright yellow mashed potatoes. I sip thick, frothy chocolate to avoid looking like a loser as I sit by myself and wait. One by one my friends plop their trays on the table.

"Hey, Linds," Raven says. Today, her thick, dark hair is coaxed into a sixties flip. With her is Emma, with gorgeous fiery hair and the eyes of a cat.

"Ladies." Gracie nods. She is the classic beauty. Straight black hair and flawless skin. She's one of the few girls in school I don't have an urge to make over.

With her is Melissa, my partner from dance team, towering over me. "Hi, guys," she says between crunches of the golden apple she's holding.

Emma and I have known each other forever. Melissa and Gracie have been friends since grade school too. Freshman year, Raven moved here from Atlanta, and she plays on the JV soccer team with Gracie. That's how we all got connected.

Once they're settled, I try to sound as casual as possible.

"So, do any of you know Noah Hornung?"

"Sure." Raven nods. "He plays hockey with my brother." Her eyes are as dark as the black coffee my dad drinks in the mornings, but somewhere in those inky irises, a glint of mischief lurks. She's on to me.

"Really?" I lean over. And immediately, I lean back in my seat, adjusting my icy blue sweater with pink-striped cuffs.

"Somebody has a crush!" Emma sings, her red curls bouncing over her broad shoulders.

I tilt my head and raise my eyebrows, unable to deny it. "So, what if I do? What do we know about this boy? Is he a total dork?"

"Drew's on the JV team, and varsity helps out a lot. Drew says Noah's really nice and helpful and stuff—not like some of the other macho varsity players," Gracie pipes in. Her narrow eyes smile like they always do when she talks about her boyfriend, Drew. "You should come to the games with me."

"Yeah! Come to the games!" Raven cheers, her bag of Cheetos letting out a whoosh as she opens it. "I always sit with my folks, which is fine, but I'd love y'all to hang out with me. Plus Noah's super cute."

"How'd you meet him?" Melissa asks, munching another bite of apple. She's the quiet one in our group. In the spring of freshman year, she confided in us that she's struggling with an eating disorder. I think she's tentative about piping in sometimes, afraid we're judging her. We're not.

"He's in youth group," adds Emma. "But I've never

seen you talk to him."

"Yeah, I thought he was." I dip a fry in ketchup. "I never had talked to him, until right before English. I know this sounds goofy. We just ran into each other in the hallway today—literally, *BOOM*—and he knew my name, which was completely surprising, and I felt something." I shake my head. "I know it sounds cheesy, but it was like we connected or something." To stop anything more ridiculous from coming out of my mouth, I pop a fry in, licking the tangy ketchup so it doesn't drip on my chin.

I look past my friends and gaze out to the chaos of the lunchroom. A group of guys including Raven's brother, Randy, is huddled around a broad-shouldered blond intently engrossed in his phone. It's the varsity hockey players. Noah stands in the back, watching his friend defeat electronic enemies, weaving his fingers through his messy hair. He looks up and sees me looking at him. I feel like grasshoppers are jumping inside my body. I drop my eyes and slurp the life out of my milkshake.

"First comes love, then comes marriage, then comes the baby in the baby carriage," Emma sings dramatically in her gorgeous voice.

I roll my eyes. "Please, God, don't let him hear Emma," I say with mock intent.

Melissa jumps in, "At least those babies have a chance at being tall, Linds."

"You might have to marry him for that reason alone," Raven adds.

About the Author

I believe in God. I believe in true love. I believe if I bang hard enough on the back of my wardrobe I'll get to Narnia someday. I believe eating chocolate is good for you. I believe part of my soul lives in France, part at the beach, and the other part in my town of Oxford, Ohio, because when I go to those places I feel at home, as if I've always belonged. I believe heaven will feel much the same. I believe God created me to be the wife of my husband, the mother of my four children, and to write the stories and speak the words He wants people to hear. I love speaking to groups and sharing His love. My other books include; *Hot*, *Angry*, *It's Complicated*, *It's Over*, and *It's Addicting*. Visit Laura L. Smith's website at: www.laurasmithauthor.com

Made in the USA
Middletown, DE
28 May 2018